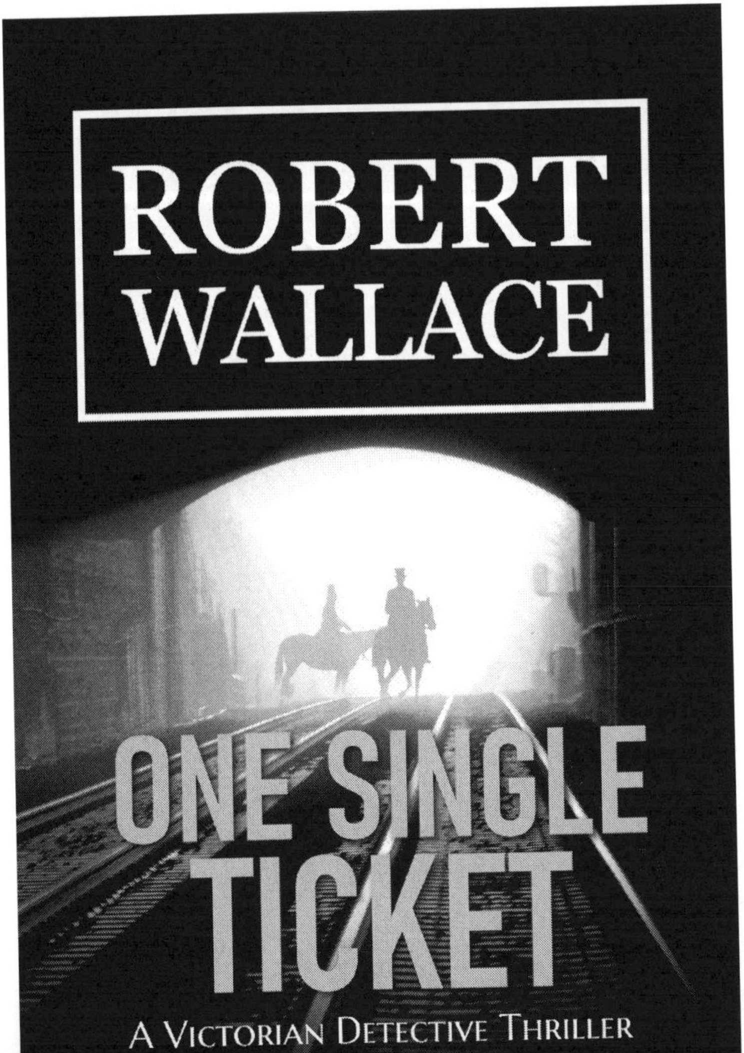
ROBERT
WALLACE
ONE SINGLE
TICKET
A VICTORIAN DETECTIVE THRILLER

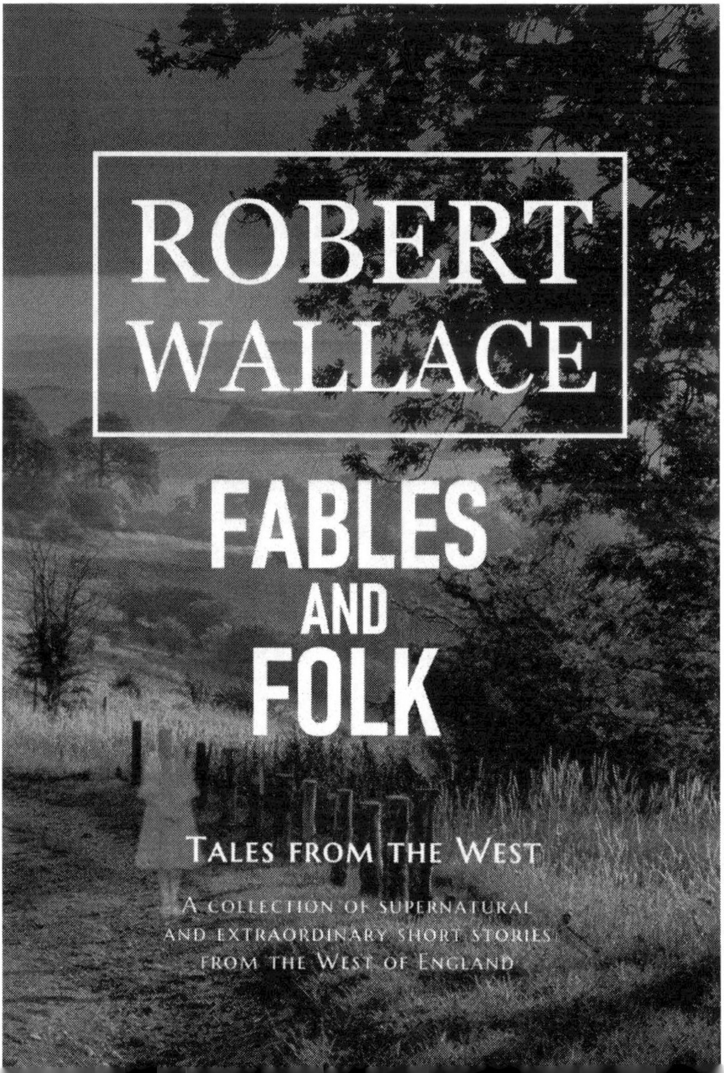
ROBERT WALLACE
FABLES AND FOLK
TALES FROM THE WEST
A COLLECTION OF SUPERNATURAL AND EXTRAORDINARY SHORT STORIES FROM THE WEST OF ENGLAND

ROBERT
WALLACE
THE BETRAYAL OF
JACQUELINE FLOWER
A PSYCHOLOGICAL CRIME THRILLER WITH
AN INTRICATE AND TWISTING STORYLINE

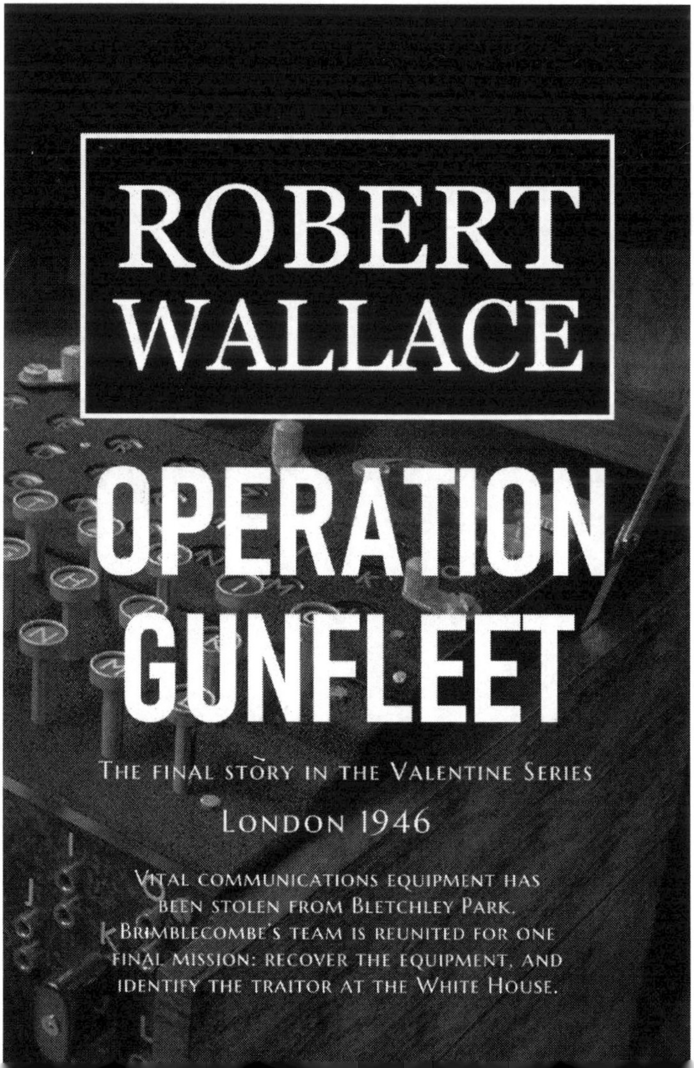
ROBERT WALLACE
OPERATION GUNFLEET
The final story in the Valentine Series
London 1946
Vital communications equipment has been stolen from Bletchley Park. Brimblecombe's team is reunited for one final mission: recover the equipment, and identify the traitor at the White House.

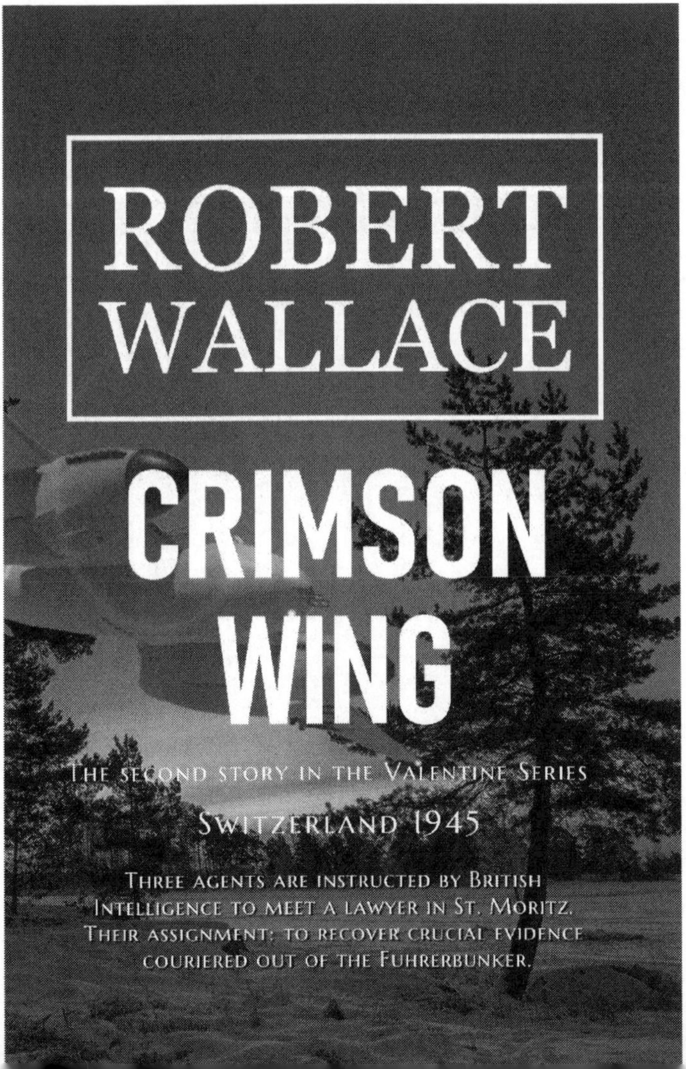
ROBERT
WALLACE
CRIMSON
WING
The second story in the Valentine Series
Switzerland 1945
Three agents are instructed by British
Intelligence to meet a lawyer in St. Moritz.
Their assignment: to recover crucial evidence
couriered out of the Fuhrerbunker.

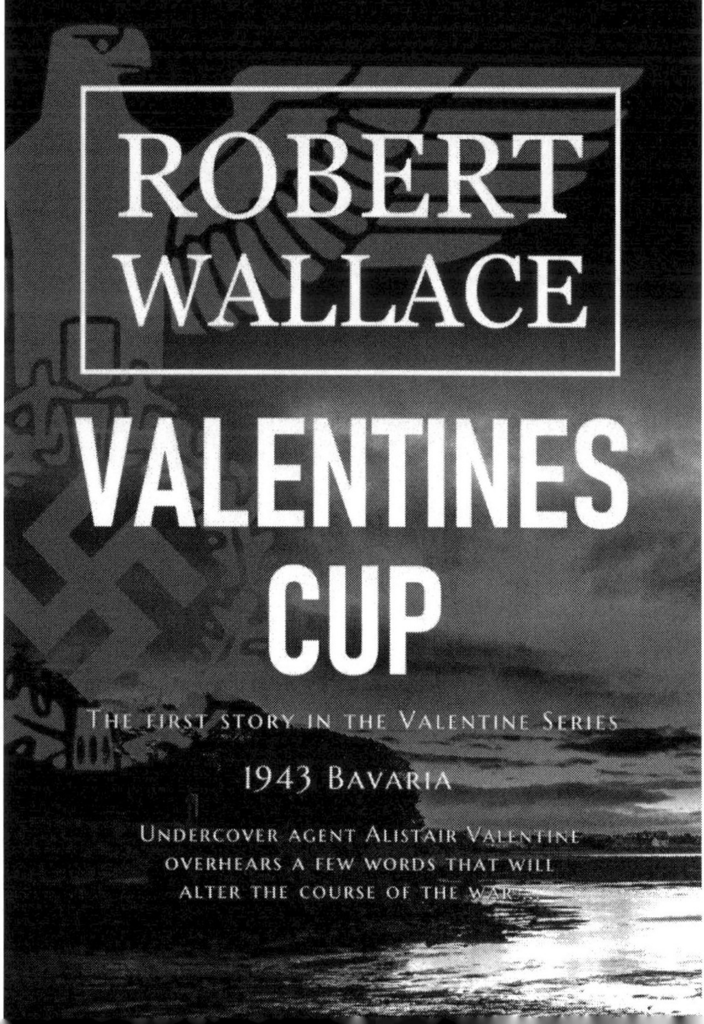
ROBERT
WALLACE
VALENTINES
CUP
THE FIRST STORY IN THE VALENTINE SERIES
1943 BAVARIA
UNDERCOVER AGENT ALISTAIR VALENTINE
OVERHEARS A FEW WORDS THAT WILL
ALTER THE COURSE OF THE WAR

Thank You

Especially to my wife Pam for her love and patience; and to Marianne, always my first and trusted reader.

To J.P. for such a great edit and providing so many creative suggestions.

Len Greenwood for the original artwork and continued enthusiasm for the Valentine Series.

Stuart Amesbury for his meticulous research and feedback.

I would also like to thank Sally Brimblecombe in France for not only being a constructive reader, but also allowing me to use her late husband's name. Nick was a great friend too but was never known as 'Brim'. That was invented purely for these stories.

It is important for me to acknowledge the on-going help and suggestions of David Kenyon, Research Historian / Bletchley Park Trust. And Robert Glasby, Curator, de Havilland Museum, London.

Also, I'd like to thank Graham Owens who helped me with Lucy's diving sequence in Scotland at the start.

There are many people in Frinton, Bristol, Bath, Portishead, Jarnac (France), Zermatt (Switzerland) and North Carolina (USA) who have also been keen proofreaders: thank you all.

And finally, to my wonderful sons James and Nibby, who have made me enormously proud. A man could not wish for a finer family. I am blessed with such good fortune..

'The last enemy.'

Richard Hillary. Macmillan and co. 1942.

ISBN 0-7126-7344-x

‘Secret Weapons – Death Rays, Doodlebugs and Churchill’s Golden Goose.’

Brian J. Ford. Osprey Publishing. 2011.

ISBN 978 1 78096 721 9

‘McIndoe’s Army – the story of the Guinea Pig Club and its indomitable members.’

Edward Bishop. Grub Street London 2001.

ISBN 1 902304 93 4

‘He was my chief – the memoirs of Adolf Hitler’s secretary.’

Christa Schroeder (Introduction by Roger Moorhouse.) Langden Müller 1985.

ISBN 978 1 84832 631 6

‘I was Hitler’s chauffeur – the memoirs of Erich Kempka.’

Erich Kempka (Introduction by Roger Moorhouse.) Kyrburg, Munich. 1951.

ISBN 978 84832 630 9

‘The wisdom of Winston Churchill – words of war and peace.’

Edited by Sean Lamb. Arcturus Publishing Ltd. 2019.

'The Debs of Bletchley Park.'

Michael Smith. Aurum Press Ltd. 2015.

ISBN 978 1 78131 388 6

'What if? Military historians imagine what might have been.'

Edited by Robert Cowley. Pan Books. 2001.

ISBN 0 330 48724 8

'The heroines of SOE – Britain's secret women in France F Section.'

Squadron Leader Beryl E. Escott. The History Press 2010.

ISBN 978 0 7524 8729 8

'The Secret life of Bletchley Park – the men and women who worked there.'

Sinclair McKay. Aurum Press Ltd. 2010.

ISBN 978 84513 633 8

'Between Silk and Cyanide – a codemaker's war 1941-1945.'

Leo Marks. Harper Collins 2000.

ISBN 0 00 710039 6

'Inside Hitler's Bunker – the last days of the Third Reich.'

'Ian Fleming and SOE's Operation Postmaster.'

Brian Lett. Pen & Sword Military 2012.

ISBN 978 178159 000 3

'The Nazis – the rise and fall of history's most evil empire.'

Paul Roland. Arcturus 2019.

ISBN 978-1-78828-483-7

'Valkyrie – the plot to kill Hitler.'

Philipp Von Boeselager. Weidenfeld & Nicolson 2009.

ISBN 978-0-297-85546-7

'Hitler's spy chief – The Wilhelm Canaris Mystery.'

Richard Bassett. Cassell Military Paperbacks. 2005.

ISBN 978-0-3043-6718-4

'Hitler's last days – an eyewitness account.'

Gerhard Boldt. Rowohlt Verlag GmBh 1947.

ISBN 0 7221 1735 3

'The secret war of Charles Fraser-Smith – the real Q of WW2.'

Charles Fraser-Smith. Michael Joseph Ltd. 1981.

ISBN 978 0 9528408 0 0

Bibliography

'They fought alone – the true story of SOE'S agents in wartime France.'

Maurice Buckmaster. Biteback Publishing Ltd. (Originally published 1958).

ISBN 978-1-84954-692-8

'A house for spies – SIS operations into occupied France from a Sussex farmhouse.'

Edward Wake-Walker. Sapere Books. 2011.

ISBN 978-1-913518-01-1

'Inside the Third Reich.'

Memoirs by Albert Speer. Published by The Macmillan Company 1970.

'Battle of Wits – the complete story of codebreaking in World War Two.'

Stephen Budiansky. Penguin Group 2000.

ISBN 0-670-88492-8

'Enigma – the battle for the code.'

Hugh Sebag-Montefiore. Weidenfeld & Nicholson 2000.

ISBN 0 297 84251 X

Permissions

I am most grateful to Anette Fuhrmeister, rights manager of the History Press in Gloucestershire, for allowing me to quote a few passages from: The Heroines of SOE (Beryl Escott) and Cloak of Enemies (Tom Keene).

to base the character of Lucy Fry.

Éliane learnt weapons handling, hand-to-hand combat, sabotage, personal survival, radio comms and disguise. Her ability to take on a convincing new identity – as Lucy had to – was a prerequisite for her role as a courier.

Many of the distinguished women of the SOE worked with the legendary cryptographer Leo Marks, whose One Time Pads probably saved many lives.

Notes from the Author

The factual background behind Monkeypuzzle.

The British Special Operations Executive (SOE) 'F' Section created a significant number of networks throughout France during World War Two. These networks – from ACOLYTE to WRESTLER – were instructed to acquire intelligence about the enemy and communicate it to SOE HQ in London. The network normally consisted of a circuit leader, a wireless operator and a courier.

MONK, also known as the MONKEYPUZZLE circuit, included a courier named Éliane Plewman. Although French, and a member of the Resistance, she was also a British agent. She was involved in many highly successful sabotage missions until she was arrested by the Gestapo and murdered by the SS in the concentration camp at Dachau.

Violette Szabo was another French/British SOE agent during WW2. On her second mission into occupied France, Szabo was captured by the German army. She was interrogated, tortured and taken to the concentration camp at Ravensbrück, where she was executed. She was posthumously awarded the George Cross, and many citations from France.

The MONKEYPUZZLE network was disbanded in 1943. Monkeypuzzle remains a compelling name; it is also a memorable title for a novel, and Éliane Sophie Browne-Bartroli –

Group Captain Miles Villiers

RAF Special Investigations Branch

José and Maria Cordera

Lucy's hosts at Residencia, López-Cordera, Spain

Dr. Orfila

Pharmacist in Villaricos, Spain

Sir Henry A. Hobson

Consul-General, Barcelona, Spain

Simon Avery

Staff member at the Barcelona Consulate, Spain

Karl Heller

Brother of Dieter

Captain Alfredo

Captain of Spanish Civil Guard, Villaricos, Spain.

Dr. Antonio Laguna and Consuela

Husband and wife medics at the Surgery, Villaricos, Spain

Bernard Valois

Pascale

BCRA agent Paris

Major-General Gubbins

Director of SOE

Commander Dieter Helle

U-boat commander, Bordeaux

Major Charles Pelham

FCO/MI6 Intelligence, Poundon

Michel and Chantal Basin

French resistance, Tarbes

'Pierre'

Radio Operator, Tarbes

Sophie Vidal

Waitress at Hôtel Maison Jaune

'Henri'

Heinrich Müller, Gestapo

Colonel John Penfold

List of Characters and Organisations

Lucy Fry
Field agent, British Intelligence.

Captains William Fairburn/Eric Sykes
Instructors at Commando Training School, Lochabar, Scotland

Freddie Valentine
Field agent, British Intelligence.

Professor Nicholas Brimblecombe
Head of British Intelligence

S/N. Sally Brooke
Staff Nurse on Ward 3. Royal Victoria Hospital, East Grinstead

Beryl Murray-Davies
Dentist at Harley Street, London.

Vera Atkins
Assistant to Col. Buckmaster

Col. Maurice Buckmaster

To Sophie. R.I. P.

I unclipped the ring from Maria's letter and knelt again to place it by the bouquet. Freddie clasped my arm, and I could see that his eyes were moist.

"That was quite something, Lucy. Maria's words ...."

"I know, Freddie. I know. And I am choking back a maelstrom of tears which I can't hold much longer ..." I folded the letter and gripped it in my hand.

"Then let them go. I'm here," Freddie said, and I collapsed into his arms, the floodgates finally open. All that pent-up emotion was released: Bordeaux, Tarbes, Villaricos, Barcelona, Skindles and now here in Arles. I don't know how long we stood there before I passed the lighter back to Freddie, and we turned to walk away.

"You will tell me the story, won't you, Lucy? Of what happened that awful night in Villaricos." Freddie asked me quietly. "How Heller nearly killed you in your bed?"

I sighed, exhausted: "You're the only one I can tell, Freddie. I have no one else."

Freddie took my arm and we walked away from the graveyard into the morning sunlight without once looking back. All the ghosts were now finally laid to rest.

THE END

came into our lives and changed us forever with your words and drawings. We will all miss your laughter and fun, including Orfila who is translating this letter for me. We are sitting in the pharmacy at the table where we all sat many times.

You will be in our hearts forever, Lucy.
Your friend, Maria.

Orfila had also written his name at the bottom of the letter. Her words were incredibly poignant and so was her gesture. I would never forget Maria either, or Antonio and Ana. But they were in the past now and I knew I had to say goodbye. I knew the family would be looked after. I delved into my coat pocket and fished out the article from Le Figaro and gazed at it one last time. I had stumbled on it in a railway station in Barcelona that day and Sophie Vidal had haunted me ever since: Waitress Slain in Arles.

"Lighter please, Freddie," I said, not turning around, not wanting to show my tears. He stepped forward and passed me an old lighter engraved with his father's name: Lt. Col. Stephen Valentine, 14th November 1916.

The page of newspaper ignited quickly in my gloved hand and the embers fell onto the marble surround of the grave, some of them glowing briefly in the light breeze before blowing away, extinguished forever. Freddie passed me the flowers and I placed

SOPHIE VIDAL

Née à Arles le 22 octobre 1920

Décédée le 7 juin 1945

À l'âge de 25 ans

Repose en Paix

I took out Maria's envelope and held it against my face before finally opening it, a million thoughts and memories racing through my mind. At the top of her letter was a fine gold eternity ring attached to the paper with a twist of wire. I read the letter out loud:

Residencia López-Cordera

Villaricos, Spain.

Dear Lucy

I can finally call you that now. I am sorry I could not visit you at Dr Laguna's surgery. Señor Garcia – the mayor of Villaricos – had to hide me and the children from Alfredo and the Falange. He knew they wanted revenge after what happened. Orfila told me that 'Henri' had murdered that poor girl in Arles. So, I am glad I warned the authorities exactly who was escaping in José's biplane. And I am glad it was shot down.

Embers

Rue Georges-Guynemer, Arles, France.

WE VISITED THE CEMETERY late the following morning when it was relatively quiet. Despite the autumn chill, a weak sun shone through the bare trees. We found the grave after making enquiries at the gatehouse: "AF 98 ROUGE," the man had said, "black marble, gold lettering, you can't miss it. Always has fresh flowers."

I walked toward the memorial and found myself shaking as I saw her name for the first time. I was dressed in black and so was Freddie. He stood dutifully behind me clutching his fedora and a bouquet. I looked down at the headstone, my tears not far away. I had rehearsed this moment a hundred times: in the bed at Dr. Laguna's, in the market at Villaricos, on the plane back with Villiers.

Now the moment was here, it felt surreal. The girl from Arles; the same age as me.

"But ... you weren't."

"No."

Freddie gripped my hand. "You feel that Müller was ultimately responsible for Tommy's incarceration and torture. And therefore, there is a connection with Arles? With Sophie?"

My eyes filled: "Yes, definitely. Tommy didn't die, thank God, but that was no thanks to Müller. He was arrested and imprisoned under his orders."

"And Müller murdered Sophie, here at the Hôtel la Maison Jaune?"

"Yes," I looked him in the eye, "of that I am sure. Müller was clearly in that newspaper picture and it's too much of a coincidence. He killed her."

Freddie nodded. He didn't ask why or what I believed the motive was. He didn't have to. He understood. It was in his eyes. It always is.

Freddie laughed: "Ha! No, I bet she wasn't. St. Mary's Paddington have 'borrowed' her from East Grinstead for three months. That number was the only way I could think of to give you a line of communication to me. At least to get a message to me via Sally."

"Yes, when I finally realised that PAD 6791 was a telephone number. Whatever made you think of such a ploy, Freddie? And cigar ash neatly concealed in the pages?"

"Brim, of course. And it was Cuban cigar ash to be precise. The idea first appeared in a Sherlock Holmes novel." Freddie liked such elaborate detail and so did Brim.

"I'm glad you gave me the number because I wanted to ask you to make this pilgrimage with me to Arles. And I didn't want anyone else to know. Not even Brim. It's too personal. It wouldn't be the same without you."

"I'm glad you asked me, Lucy. But this is not just about Sophie Vidal, is it?" Freddie asked and looked me in the eye. We were sharing a bottle of white Rhône wine and a little pot of olives. Despite his presence, I was in a peculiarly reflective mood. Probably because of what we had to do the next day.

"No." I took his hand. "It's also about a very brave man, codename 'Seahorse' – Tommy – he was an SOE agent based in Paris. Arrested and tortured by the Gestapo. I didn't know this until the meeting at Skindles when Brim told me. I never met Seahorse. I was supposed to, but they got to him before I had the

L'arlésienne
(The girl from Arles)

The Artisan Bar, Arles, France.

"WHEN DID YOU REALISE the Georges Simenon novel wasn't from Brim?" Freddie asked me, with a cunning expression. The Artisan Bar in the centre of Arles was absolutely packed with tourists from all over Europe. Some sort of music festival we gathered, judging by the numerous posters. And the number of violin and cello cases stuffed into every corner of the noisy bar.

"Not for ages. In fact, it was while I was convalescing at Dr. Laguna's Surgery that the penny finally dropped. But I couldn't think of anyone who lived in Paddington. Not even Brim: so you kept me guessing."

Freddie chuckled: "Good, Lucy old thing. I like to keep you guessing."

"When I got put through to the Anaesthetics office on that direct line you gave me, it was Sally Brooke who answered. I

"All right. But no photo."

"Understood."

Valois scribbled the address down on a piece of hotel paper: Cimetière de Trinquetaille – rue Georges-Guynemer.

"You know where this is? Not far from the river?" He handed the piece of paper to Lucy.

"Thank you, I am sure we can find it, Monsieur. Enjoy the rest of the game."

Valois grunted as they turned and walked away.

the paper. As a mark of respect. Maybe take a photograph?"

"No photograph." He was emphatic; but why?

"As you wish, monsieur. Of course. But I'd still like to take some flowers."

"I don't think so. You didn't even know her. And neither did anyone at your paper."

The door opened, and Freddie came in, took off his fedora and smiled at Valois politely. He made a noise to indicate how cold it was out in the courtyard, clapping his gloved hands together.

"Are you a newspaper photographer?" Valois asked Freddie suspiciously.

"No."

"My fiancé," said Lucy. "He came for the ride."

"Pah. Long and unnecessary, if you ask me," said Valois, glancing at Freddie indignantly, as if he resented his presence.

Freddie's French was as good as Lucy's. "Sorry, we'll have to go now, darling. Our table is booked for six. We don't want to miss the overture of 'L'Arlésienne.' Monsieur Bizet would be offended." He inclined his head towards Valois. "My apologies."

"If Monsieur Bizet was alive, yes." Lucy smiled coquettishly.

Valois smiled briefly at the comment, giving the vaguest hint of concession that he accepted that Freddie might be the girl's fiancé and not some disreputable newspaper photographer. From Paris. So, Lucy pleaded one last time:

"Monsieur?" Lucy could look most appealing when the

Valois. I don't question what the editor tells me to do. I just do my job."

"There's nothing to say." Valois turned to pick up a glass of Ricard from behind the bar. He lit a Gauloise. "They came here lording it over us humble provincials and left. The courtyard out there is lovely in the summer, shaded by the trees. We are lucky. It was the perfect venue for such an occasion." He glanced through the window and noticed Freddie but said nothing.

"I see." Lucy picked up her documents, apparently resigned to the fact she would get no further.

"And the police never caught Sophie's killer. That's what is important, not a flying visit by a couple of eccentrics who just love the limelight."

"What was he like, this man?" asked Lucy warily. "It says he lived here."

"I don't know ... I ... I don't know if I even met him." Lucy sensed Valois was lying. Surely he would have vetted the man his niece was sharing her room with. Particularly given the age difference. Something was not right.

She waited. Valois turned back to listen to the game, drank his Ricard and finished his cigarette. She could feel his discomfort. Could Müller have paid him off, she wondered? Was that even conceivable? His own niece?

"Monsieur, I have an idea. Is there a memorial for your niece somewhere here in Arles?"

Valois turned, scratched his unshaven chin and eyed her:

your courtyard." Her voice sounded husky and breathless. She pointed at the window.

"Oh, them? Pourcel didn't do Arles any favours." He all but spat out the words. "Or Van Gogh either, for that matter."

"But the publicity for La Maison Jaune must have been positive and ..."

Valois cut her off again: "The only real publicity was for those two self-serving barbouilleurs from Paris. Somebody murdered my niece, Sophie. That's the real news. Look, that's her. The waitress." He pointed a stubby, nicotine-stained finger at the pretty girl in the picture.

"Oh, I'm sorry. I had no way of knowing that girl was your niece. Nobody told me." Lucy looked down at her feet, as if ashamed.

"Doesn't it say?"

Arles had another chance at goal, and the sound was building again from the frantic home crowd.

"No."

"But you knew she was murdered? Here in my hotel? In her room? Look at the headline," Valois said. He sounded a little unconvincing. Lucy wondered if he was hiding something.

"Yes. I read the whole article many times on the train down from Paris. But there was no mention that she was your niece, Monsieur. None. Anyway, the surname is not the same."

Valois laughed: "You came all this way to write about those two showoffs? What a complete waste of time. Damned

walked on ahead of her to wait. It was deserted; the tables and chairs had been stacked awaiting the arrival of spring. Inside, the hotel was enlivened only by the sound of a football match on the radio in the bar, and the place looked tired and run down. The stoutly built man behind the reception desk eyed Lucy with undisguised suspicion. She gave him the smile that always worked.

"Can I help you?" asked Bernard Valois in a chesty timbre that suggested he was no stranger to strong tobacco. Some of his attention seemed to be distracted by the commentary from the bar. Lucy placed her identity card on the counter, and he glanced at it briefly. "We're not hiring," he said rudely. Then she produced a letter from the editor of Le Figaro in Paris introducing her as Claude Moreau: a journalist, living in Clignancourt.

"I'm not looking," said Lucy coquettishly, in her excellent French. She took out the crumpled Figaro newspaper article with its accompanying photograph and put it on the counter too. Valois studied it, looking pained. He shook his head. "You recall this feature, Monsieur?"

"Of course I recall it. What do you want?" He was listening intently to the radio; a goal had been scored by the Arles team and the crowd was going wild. She assumed her most innocent expression, pouting to make her lips fuller and more sensual, leaning in towards him so he could savour her scent. And enjoy her closeness.

Valois

Hôtel la Maison Jaune, Arles, France.

LUCY FRY WAS BY no means perfect - she had never thought she was – quite the reverse if anything. She could be positively ungainly if she didn't make the effort. She wasn't a natural athlete, she had to work hard to keep fit and remain physically agile. She was supremely headstrong. It was these qualities that made her who she was. She was striking to look at with a symmetrical face, blue eyes, full lips and high cheekbones. Her skin, kissed by the Spanish sun, revealed fine laughter lines around her eyes when she smiled. Which she did often; a look of detached amusement was her natural expression. Except when she was angry, then her eyes turned to fire. That it was best not to cross her, was the unspoken consensus.

She approached the front gates of Hôtel la Maison Jaune and opened one of them cautiously. Her heart was pounding because here, within these walls, was the ghost she had to face: who had deeply affected her life and, indirectly, the lives of many others.

him.

Freddie Valentine kept a straight face and looked at Brim, Penfold and Villiers, but not at me. My heart melted at the sight of him.

"I used to know this delightful nurse at East Grinstead, called Lucy Fry. Has anybody seen her?" His voice, ironic and smooth, was so familiar.

I shot out of my chair and ran towards him: "She's here, Freddie," I said, bursting into tears. There was nothing in the world I could do to stop them.

"I thought I might find you here," said Freddie, winking at Brim.

in Paris. On headed notepaper, with the correct address of the newspaper and all the relevant telephone numbers and telegram details." I paused. "The letter should introduce me as Claude Moreau, same as my CNI ..." I took out my identity card "with my address in Paris – 23b rue Ramey, Clignancourt. I take it that address is still valid?"

"Yes," said Brim. "A former SOE safe house, still intact. May I ask why you need this document?"

I tried to look my most appealing and Villiers finally smiled. "No. All I ask is that you trust me. Nothing to do with the Service. This is personal. And it's vital to my sanity."

"Yes, of course, Lucy. I'll get on to it in the morning." He took out his pocketbook and I could see him making a note. "When do you need it?"

"In a week? I can pop into the Firs when I get back from Devon, as easy as pie."

"Consider it done." Brim glanced at his watch as a grandfather clock struck seven somewhere out in the corridor. There was a light tap on the door and it opened to admit a tall man with a very slight limp. He wore a beautiful charcoal-grey suit with a cashmere overcoat draped over his shoulders. Clutching his fedora, he peered at the group as if lost. It was such a shock that I just could not believe my eyes. He could have walked straight off a Hollywood film set with his fair hair, blue-grey eyes, sun-tanned features and smile which electrified the room.

was somehow distracted – or maybe she distracted him – and she certainly cracked him over the head with a wine bottle."

My mind raced. "But you and Orfila said there was no murder weapon in the kitchen."

"She swept up the pieces of glass and buried them in the garden," said Villiers, smiling, "before she came running down the road to find us. She must have known you were alive. And she had just about enough time to bury the incriminating evidence. It's a big garden."

"How do you know this for certain?" I must have sounded doubtful.

"Because that was what she told Orfila in the truck outside the villa, at the time. He thought she was talking a lot of nonsense at first, but she wanted him to know that it was her who killed him and not you. Maria was not as drunk as she pretended to be. In fact, she was a talented actress and had us all fooled."

She certainly did. I looked down at my bag, almost tempted to tear open that bloody envelope, but I didn't. I knew the truth now and that was all that mattered. But I did have a question and I needed to ask it now. So I decided to change the subject completely:

"Brim. Could one of your boffins at the Toy Shop concoct a little deceptive something for me?"

Brim pursed his lips again and his expression melted into a smile. "What did you have in mind?" There was a faint air of

"I remember seeing him – did he betray me to Heller's brother?"

The pieces of that blessed jigsaw puzzle in my brain fitted together now – the civil servant with a bag of tools and an expression which should have made me suspicious. He'd bugged Hobson's office, looking for an opportunity to make some money and found it in me. Selling confidential information to the enemy: he had heard everything I'd confided to Hobson, including the fact that I lived in Villaricos, although I don't remember giving him the address. Bloody hell, yes! A lesson.

Brim chuckled, "If it's any consolation – in a macabre way – Avery's body was found in a railway station cloakroom in Bordeaux." He paused, serious now. "He had been fatally stabbed with a stiletto. Witnesses at the Hôtel de Normandie remembered a kerfuffle in the lounge between a disfigured man and someone else, but they couldn't remember much about the second man, other than he was well-dressed. We know a Karl Heller bought a return ticket from Paris to Bordeaux: he was obliged to produce identity."

I tried again to recollect that night in the kitchen at Villaricos. My left hand shot up to my chest; I could feel the lumpy nodules and scar tissue through the material of my blouse.

"I didn't kill my attacker, Brim, I am sure of that. But the honest thing is, I simply don't remember. I was running away; it's just all..."

"So, it doesn't matter who pulled the trigger, John," said Brim. "The fact is that it was pulled. The biplane was shot down. Müller is dead, and here is Lucy, alive and well. Correct?"

My head spun. Maria? That scatty, apparently simple country girl had done all that on her own? Sacrificed her brother to kill Heinrich Müller, the head of the Gestapo?

I was still clutching that blessed envelope. I slipped it discreetly back into my bag, tucking it right down near the bottom as if to bury it. I had no idea what was in it, but now was not the time to open it. When I looked up, I noticed Brim watching me. He gave me a curious smile.

Brim said, "There's a suite booked here for you tonight, Lucy. And in the morning, my chauffeur will drive you down to Devon."

My parents. Yes, that would be wonderful. I'd missed them. I wondered how my mother would be.

Brim smiled kindly. "Your father would appreciate it, I am sure."

"That's more than kind, Brim, so thoughtful." I dried my eyes with the back of my hand. So, Brim had spoken to my father. I could sense there was something else.

"I need to ask you one last question."

"Fire away," I said, wondering.

Brim took a first sip of his single malt: "Does the name Simon Avery mean anything to you?" That name again! I narrowed my eyes and looked at Villiers, then shook my head.

"Why didn't you tell me?" I snapped at him.

Brim looked at me kindly. "Instructions from me, Lucy. Don't blame Villiers. We needed to give Snr García the opportunity to have Alfredo arrested by the National Guard."

I reached into my bag and pulled out the envelope from Maria. "Is that what's in here? That Maria made the call to Garcia?" I asked Villiers.

"I don't know what Maria wrote in her letter, Lucy," said Villiers, quite reasonably. "I haven't read it. Only Dr. Orfila and Maria know what it says. Why don't you open the damned thing and find out?"

"That's enough," said Brim. Did he realise how sensitive the contents might be? Was Brim really that perceptive, or was he just being careful?

Penfold stepped in. "This Maria may have raised the alarm with Snr García, but who shot the plane down?"

"That's a key question," said Brim, with a twist of mischief. He paused: "But in the end, the answer doesn't really matter. Villiers, if you please?"

Villiers sank his malt in one gulp and chased it with some Guinness. He looked at Brim and then directly at me:

"The night Orfila and I came to rescue you at the villa, Lucy, I missed a radio transmission from an RT operator called Rosie at SIB/NORTH/CRANWELL. She was going to confirm that a biplane had been shot down in Tangier, and thousands of US dollars recovered from a fireproof safe with a file listing all the

Then he opened the innings with the fast spinner I was expecting. "I know you are shocked about Paris, Lucy. But I want you to concentrate on yourself. Bordeaux was a fantastic coup – for you – for the Service. Extraordinary achievement ..." He paused ...

"Thank you. It was my job."

He ignored my glib response: "But I want to turn to Spain. Is that alright?"

Villiers and Penfold looked at each other with vague discomfort at my dismissive words. I hadn't meant to sound rude. I composed myself: "Yes, Brim."

"Maria Cordera made the call," he said, inhaling deeply on his cigarette. "She went to Señor García, the Mayor of Villaricos and explained that her brother was helping a senior Nazi executioner to escape to Morocco. And had probably helped many others too."

"Maria?" I was dumbfounded. I downed my drink in an unladylike fashion.

"Captain ...?" Brim looked across at Villiers for a name.

"Alfredo," supplied Villiers, on cue.

"Captain Alfredo, yes. Local police chief. He was in on the whole caper. Maria knew her only chance was Señor García. He's anti-Fascist and he accepted her story." Brim looked at me for a response.

"Did you know about this, Villiers?" I asked accusingly. I was livid.

the lounge. He looked disappointed and, just for a moment, I felt a little sorry for him. But only a little. The break had done me good and the fresh air had rejuvenated me. The ghosts of the past were back in their places. For now.

Brim was still sitting in the same chair. I could see he was itching to ask me questions in the mission debrief, but that wasn't his style. He would deliver a well-aimed ball like a fast bowler and wait for the wicket to fly. But what on earth could it be?

The story about Tommy had shaken us all. We were now two hours into our high tea and Penfold was speaking with animation about his time in Berlin working with the Americans and Russians – "Mavis couldn't stand it, of course. On the first plane back to London! Didn't like the food, didn't like the accommodation. Most of all, she couldn't stand the Americans: 'boisterous' is what she called them! I ask you!"

"Not the word I'd use to describe General Pritchard – 6th US Army Group," said Villiers, mimicking a plausible Texan accent.

"Now, now," said Brim in playful admonishment.

He stood, went over to a cabinet and poured small measures of single malt into four crystal tumblers, and I could see from the other men's faces what a rare treat this must be. He delivered them to the table, sat back down and lit a Senior Service with his traditional Ronson. He handed me a tumbler and motioned to the others to help themselves. The crystal felt heavy in my hand and the whisky was delicious, a perfect sequel after the

Debrief

Skindles Hotel, Maidenhead, England.

I WANDERED THROUGH THE French windows into a small walled garden and took a few deep breaths. The evening was warm and still; no sounds of crickets and mosquitoes buzzing in the air. And no Mediterranean aromas to tickle my tastebuds. A few days ago, I had been in the dusty dry town of Villaricos and now it was lush green Buckinghamshire. My mind raced back to the café near the Gare du Nord and the decision I had made there to return to England. I don't know how long I stood there with a million thoughts and memories. How I longed for a good night's sleep without nightmares; without the memory of being attacked so viciously and the tragedy of Sophie Vidal.

"Lucy?" It was Villiers. "Are you all right?"

"Yes." He almost succeeded in hiding the fact that he knew I'd been crying.

"I'll come back in," I said, discreetly wiping a tear away.

Villiers made to come over and – what – comfort me? I

time.”

"Christ," said Penfold, grey-faced. Even Villiers was quiet for once.

"When he finally reached Chemnitz, after being captured by a German patrol and escaping once again, he gave his American interrogators details of all the German troops and battery locations which he'd seen en route."

"What a man," I said softly to myself. That is real courage.

Brim continued, "He set out for Paris in a car driven by two friends and, although they were fired on by German patrols, with typical Tommy timing he arrived there on VE day. So that's one bit of good news."

"And he made it back?" asked Penfold.

"Yes. His report finally reached London via the Americans, by which time he'd escaped. On 8 May he flew back to England."

"What will happen to him?" I asked. It had been a gruelling story to hear. I still felt illogically guilty I hadn't met him as planned.

Brim regarded me carefully. Again, it felt as if he knew what I was thinking. And yes, what I was feeling. He continued: "If his health holds up, he'll testify, possibly at Nuremberg. A lot of the captured Nazis will deny what happened – and many have escaped, as you well know. So that's it, Lucy. You wanted to know."

"Yes. Thank you, I did."

"I say, Brim," said Penfold, "shall we have a break for ten minutes? I quite fancy a spot of fresh air. And I'm sure Miss Fry

“Are you sure you want to hear about such brutality on a joyous day like this?”

I thought for a moment. “Yes, because I was supposed meet him and didn’t."

“Couldn’t,” snapped Brim with uncharacteristic fervour. He steepled his fingers and looked at the others, as if deciding how much to reveal. Villiers and Penfold seemed riveted as Brim continued. “We know this because he told us. He was taken to Buchenwald concentration camp where he witnessed the most appalling brutality. He’s alive but has aged about twenty years. So, at least you know that before I explain what happened. He is commonly known within the service as Tommy.”

I could feel a hot tear run down my cheek. Brim went on to say that despite the torture he’d suffered at the hands of the Gestapo in Paris, Tommy had maintained his cover story that he was Squadron Leader Dodkin, and the Germans knew him as such when he arrived at the camp. He escaped by convincing the German officer in charge of injecting prisoners with typhus that if he allowed him and twenty-one other prisoners to escape, then he would testify on his behalf at his war-crimes trial. Yes, I can see you are shocked. All of you.”

“And the officer believed him?” I asked quietly.

Brim nodded gravely: “Tommy was injected with a harmless liquid instead of the deadly typhus and was smuggled out of Buchenwald. He was then sent to other camps, but on 16 April he escaped from a train bound for Czechoslovakia when it

the heart if I hadn't rolled over. I tried to smile, my natural default.

"And I gather this Dr. Laguna was happy for you to fly?"

"Yes," I said and looked at Villiers, who handed Brim an envelope. The invoice for my treatment I surmised; not very subtle. "Yes, thank you. He was."

Brim gave me a look I had seen before: "You have a question, don't you? Not about this meeting, here today. Something else?"

Sometimes Brim's perception was uncanny; it was as if he could read my mind: "Yes, I do. Is it appropriate to raise the question now?"

Brim looked around: "You are among trusted friends and colleagues. What's on your mind?"

I took a deep breath. "What happened to Seahorse, the man I was supposed to meet in Paris? I'd like to know. After everything that's happened it's a missing link, if you get my drift."

Brim sighed and pursed his lips, as he did when marshalling his thoughts. "Your report based on what your contact in Paris – Pascale – surmised, was correct. Flight Lieutenant Yeo- Thomas – Seahorse – had gone to Passy station on the morning of the twenty-first to meet another agent and been arrested by the Germans. He was taken to Gestapo HQ and tortured to the point of death. I'll spare you further details, for the moment."

"God."

"But we don't think he was betrayed; it was probably just bad timing."

award, I wondered facetiously? What would it be? He stood politely and inclined his head.

"May I introduce you to Colonel John Penfold, the Berlin Resident?" asked Brim. I noticed a pipe in the ashtray with a chamois tobacco pouch beside it. So that was the source of the pungent aroma I had detected.

"Enchanted to meet you at last, Miss Fry," said Penfold. He twitched his nose like a curious hamster, "I have heard so much about you. And I've seen the evidence of your artistic talents." He smiled politely and sat down again.

Brim was wearing a double-breasted dark blue blazer and grey trousers, with a shirt and cravat, and looked as immaculate as ever. Penfold was similarly garbed but couldn't pull it off with Brim's understated elegance. Brim rubbed his hands together and pointed at the table like a magician.

"Do sit, Lucy. And Villiers, over there next to John, if you please. Now, the hotel has done its level best to put on a decent spread – it would seem to have a cordial arrangement with local farmers. What can I pass you?"

"I'll try a bottle of Guinness please, Brim, since the baby is asleep," I said laughing, "and one of everything else. I'm famished. We haven't eaten a thing since Paris, and that was only a stale airport croissant and some undrinkable slime they were trying to pass off as tea."

Brim slapped his thigh: "Ha! I knew you would! It's so good to see you, Lucy. How's the wound?"

at the Savoy. 'My God,' I thought. 'What am I in for now?'

*

Brim arose from his seat at a table laden with plates of sandwiches and several bottles of Guinness. I smiled and shook his outstretched hand and was suddenly overwhelmed by a barrage of conflicting emotions. The last time I had seen him was before my mission to Bordeaux. And his warning – watch your back – had prepared me for the mock Gestapo-style kidnapping I had experienced at Beaulieu. This had, in turn, probably been the reason I had survived the encounter with Heller in my bedroom in Villaricos. Once again, he retained his grip of my hand.

"God, but it's good to see you!" He positively beamed, and I nearly cried. Brim was a complex man, but I could see that his jubilant greeting was heartfelt. If Villiers and another man hadn't been present, I would have hugged him and I sensed Brim felt the same. I had to bounce back with a Lucy witticism to disguise my emotion:

"Guinness is for new mothers isn't it, Brim? Plenty of iron and minerals!" Suddenly I felt rejuvenated, the plane journey from Spain a distant memory.

He smiled with genuine pleasure: "Welcome home, Lucy. We've missed you. Villiers, good afternoon to you too."

"Brim," said Villiers a little formally.

Skindles

Skindles Hotel, Maidenhead, England.

SKINDLES HOTEL IN MAIDENHEAD, I had heard, was a former coaching inn and a fashionable rendezvous for assignations of all sorts: amorous, social and commercial. Outside it were elegant cars, and people who were stylishly dressed and seemed too young to be retired, and too smart to have been recently de-mobbed. A concierge and several porters were busy assisting guests with their luggage. I followed Villiers through the plush reception area and down a long-carpeted corridor to the Bridge Room. The hotel smelt of wood polish, expensive perfume and tobacco smoke. We arrived at a pair of tall, oak-panelled doors to which a sign had been attached:

PRIVATE MEETING. DO NOT DISTURB.

Villiers tapped once.

"Come." I knew that voice at once, that solitary, emphatic

by an RAF staff car and driven off the airbase along the A40 towards Oxford. I wasn't told our destination or who we were meeting, although I had a pretty shrewd idea about the latter. The car was a battleship-grey Humber: brand new, complete with chauffeur who I suspected was an armed British Intelligence employee. He most certainly had the build for it. I was asleep by the time we reached Gerrard's Cross. When I awoke, I felt unpleasantly groggy and slightly disorientated.

west of London. At least the fields and farms below looked lush and green, unlike the arid land of southern Spain. I suddenly shivered. Was it the thought of the cold weather below us, or something else?

Villiers was buckled in beside me reading a stack of newspapers; some old, some very recent. The main stories seemed to be the American atomic attacks on Japan and their subsequent surrender. There were also many pictures of Hitler and Dönitz, the ruins of Berlin. And many articles describing the situation in the United States and the disarray in London. Villiers had been silent for most of the journey, either absorbed in the papers or dozing. Even during the refueling stop in Paris he had said very little. I couldn't be bothered to read news. I felt I had been too close to the reality of it, especially in France. My mind was in a whirl and I couldn't settle.

How sad to think I would never see Orfila again to drink coffee, eat his almond pastries and improve my conversational Spanish. His English was already more or less perfect. What a good friend he had been to me. I couldn't have made the journey to Barcelona without him; that was for certain, given the prejudice against women travelling alone. Maria and the children were also lost to me, their fate a mystery. That part of my life, and those people, were gone forever. I knew I would never return to Villaricos.

The Lysander clunked down onto the runway at just after three in the afternoon. By the time we had disembarked, with

Northolt

RAF Northolt, London, England.

SIX WEEKS AFTER MY admission to Dr. Laguna's surgery – late August '45 - I was free to be discharged. They had been extremely kind to me and nursed me back to health. I had made the telephone call to the Paddington number in London, on the pretext that I needed to call my father in Devon. It was a shock to hear the voice of the person who answered ...

As the Westland Lysander aircraft descended for its final approach into RAF Northolt, I thought to myself, how typical – rain and drizzle. What a lousy welcome home to England. The truth is, I am not a good flyer, I suppose it's because I have no control over my destiny. My father would have said it's because I am obstinate; I had scowled all the way from Hurn Airport to Jersey once – not very far. But this journey from Spain had been long and turbulent, and the bumpiness made my queasy.

I wiped the condensation from the tiny window and peered out at the mist and rain. We seemed to be descending anti-

while on the voyage back: 67,91. They had been subconsciously puzzling me for days as I lay in that bed in search of answers. And then it clicked. Of course! It was a telephone number! How silly I had been not to see it. And the inscription in the front was a three-digit letter prefix for a part of London: P.A.D. It had to be Paddington 6791. Except I knew Brim lived in Pimlico, near the Thames. Not Paddington. Maybe it was a British Intelligence safe house. There was only one way to find out. I sniffed the pages again; the same stale cigar ash was pervasive and had smudged at the seam.

Three or four days would buy me some time. My convalescence was nearly over. I needed the opportunity to stroll – perhaps with Consuela – around to the post office in the square. And this time, I wouldn't be calling a Bar-Tabac near Tarbes. It would be the operator in London. And who would answer Paddington 6791? That was a question I couldn't wait to be answered.

"We can wait," offered Villiers hopefully.

"That won't be necessary," said Laguna. "You may come back tomorrow. I think Miss Fry will be fit enough to travel in three or four days." His tone was formal.

I smiled meekly at Villiers and Orfila. There we are then, doctor's orders! Three or four more days to recover sounded fine to me. A thought occurred:

"Orfila, could you get something from the residencia for me, please?"

"Of course, Jovencita. His old eyes sparkled, delighted to be asked, to be involved.

"Next to my bed is a book by Georges Simenon. You can't miss it. I need to keep my French up to speed."

"Of course," he said again. "Anything else?"

I thought of my sketch pad and the drawing of Maria I had planned to give her as a present. It was, perhaps, too risqué for Orfila's eyes: "No, just the book is fine, thank you."

Dr. Laguna, Orfila and Villiers left me in peace to gaze at the ceiling fan once again. I was still clutching the envelope containing Maria's letter. I would read it, but not now. Maybe back in London on a cold, wet winter's afternoon. Or maybe in Devon at my father's cottage. Or maybe never. As the door closed and Laguna placed the BP cuff on my arm again, I thought once more of that poor girl. Sophie Vidal. And in that moment, I made myself a silent promise.

Within an hour, the Simenon book was in my hands. Orfila

with a cover up."

"So do we, Lucy. But nothing can be proved. The deal is, if Alfredo says we can go, we go, and go as soon as possible. The aircraft is ready when you are. It's been back to England twice for a change of crew – duty rosters and so on – since you were admitted here," Villiers explained with his customary precision. Maybe he actually was a lawyer in another world outside the Service.

Orfila had been looking at me as a father might look at his poorly daughter. "How do you feel, Jovencita?"

I sensed a conspiracy between them. I was sure of one thing: "I'm not opening this letter," I said again. They both looked at me with an expression that said, 'stubborn so-and-so' and I shrugged. I waited for a few moments before answering Orfila's question. "I feel well enough to go back to London," I said finally, "since you ask. I've had my stitches out and I'm more or less all right. How long is the flight? I'm not a terribly good traveller."

Villiers took my arm; it was a familiar gesture from a nebulous memory. When had he done that before? Was I conscious at the time? In any event, he didn't answer my question. "We saved your life, Lucy. The stiletto wound was deep. You were bleeding to death." He paused for a moment. "Who was he, your attacker? "

I felt sick. So that was what had happened. But what of Maria? Did she kill Heller? She was frail and drunk; how could she have managed it? Was that the deal with Alfredo?

Villiers intervened in his courtroom manner – could he not even tone it down for a sickroom? "Lucy, you must understand this is a serious situation. An unknown man, carrying no identification, breaks into your bedroom and tries to kill you. This was no accident; this was attempted murder. That man later dies of a massive trauma to the head and there is a knife wound to his upper shoulder."

I gave a noncommittal nod. So, Heller was dead then. But I hadn't killed him, had I?

Villiers continued: "There is no murder weapon. No distinguishable fingerprints on the kitchen knife. Plenty of smeared blood. Maria doesn't remember anything – and neither do you." He waited for my response, but it was almost as if he knew the answer.

I said nothing.

"You couldn't have killed that man, you'd passed out. I saw the crime scene," said Villiers, "and so did Dr. Orfila. We went to the residencia because Brim feared for your safety ... does the name Simon Avery ring a bell?"

I shook my head.

"That's why Maria has gone." Villiers's explanation sounded hollow. What had Maria done? Something wasn't right, but I couldn't quite articulate why it all felt so uncomfortable. "Captain Alfredo of the police has agreed to let you go," Villiers continued.

"That's very big of him," I said, more sarcastically than I had

Dr. Laguna and Consuela removed my stitches two days later. The procedure was carried out like an operation, with sterilised instruments, theatre-style drapes, hot water and surgical spirit. At the end of the process, it was pronounced a success. I nearly cried; their kindness had been wonderful, and I am sure I'm not the easiest of patients. In fact I know I am not. My father would have agreed with that. He had once nursed me through tonsilitis as a child and said later I had been 'tiresome'. An expression I had never forgotten.

*

There was a hesitant knock on the door and Orfila and Villiers stepped solemnly into my room like a couple of undertakers. Orfila clutched a sealed envelope and handed it over to me without any form of greeting. "From Maria," he said, looking profoundly guilty.

"You're not saying she wrote this?" They both looked at me expectantly, hoping to see me tear the envelope open. But I didn't. God only knows what secrets had been divulged in those lines of prose.

"She dictated it to me in Spanish. I translated it and wrote it down. So, yes you are right, Lucy. Open it." Orfila spoke firmly. But there was an edge to his voice that was mysterious.

"No. What does it say? Let me guess. She didn't have time to visit me. Why?" I was damned well hurt if the truth be known. I continued: “Mr. Villiers wondered if he could visit you. Dr. Orfila has enquired about you two or three times a day.” Before I could answer, Consuela placed a thermometer under my tongue and we all waited until she withdrew it and made her pronouncement: “37.7 degrees. So, no fever. This is good. It means there is no infection in your wound. We have been – what is the word? – scrupulous with hygiene.” She shook the thermometer as we nurses always do.

“Your visitors?" asked Laguna, knitting his brows together once more. “When?”

“After my stitches are out, please, Dr. Laguna.” He nodded and they both withdrew from my room. It didn’t occur to me to ask who was paying for such attentive service.

I knew the identity of my attacker of course, but I could not divulge that knowledge to anyone except Brim. I didn’t know how much Villiers knew of my mission to Bordeaux; and I could not tell Orfila and the local police the truth, which surely must be covered by the Official Secrets Act. I couldn’t remember what had happened to Heller that night; my mind was a blank. I remembered him attacking me in my room; and I remembered running away from him in fear – right through the residencia – down to the kitchen. I recalled trying to comfort Maria. But what on earth happened to Heller? I decided that the fewer questions I asked, the better. Let them tell me, if they knew. I spent a few more days trying to piece that night together, but fragments were always missing. I thought it strange that I hadn’t heard

water and pulled the bed sheet down from my upper body. For some reason I expected to see blood-soaked bandages, but all I could see was a single dressing, ten inches square, taped to my upper chest area. She passed me the glass. I sat up awkwardly on one elbow and drained it. The water was cool and thirst quenching, and I settled back. Dr. Laguna raised my left arm, slipped on the blood pressure cuff and inflated it. He put on his stethoscope and listened. There was the familiar whoosh any nurse knew very well. He sighed with satisfaction and slipped off the cuff.

"120 over 80. Perfect," said Laguna. "It was 90 over 60 when you were admitted here at the surgery: very low from blood loss and shock." He asked if I remembered the oranges and I think I frowned. He pointed at a waste bin and told me it was full of orange peel and tomato stalks. "You've eaten twenty oranges and as many tomatoes. And litres of water with your salt tablets. Your body craved Vitamin C, salt and water to re-hydrate you. If only we could combine that into one magic solution, somebody would become very rich." Dr. Laguna had bushy black eyebrows which met in the middle when he frowned. He reminded me of a fox, and I couldn't get the image out of my mind. I must have sniggered. "Something is funny, Lucy?" He frowned as he asked me, and his brows knitted together once again.

"No. And no, I don't remember eating that lot." My eyes glanced toward the waste bin, but the rest of me wouldn't move. It was too painful and difficult to turn when I was lying down.

But why kill Sophie? He was having an affair with her. More than that, according to the article, he was sharing her room at the hotel: a forty-five-year-old man with a twenty-five-year-old girl. Maybe she had seen something incriminating and he had no choice but to kill her. But what could it have been? I strained to engage my brain. He was escaping from Germany. What if there were other Nazis on the run from the occupying forces? What if Sophie had stumbled by accident upon a list of senior Nazi officials willing to pay for freedom? I painstakingly followed my own train of thought, robbed of my usual quickness. Antonio López and José Cordera were friends, and José was in The Falange Española. They flew aircraft, they had a crash and Antonio was killed. So, José and Müller had to rebuild another biplane to escape to Tangier; except that it was shot down. By whom?

There was a soft tap on my door, which opened to admit a tall man wearing a long white coat with a stethoscope around his neck and a sphygmomanometer in his hand.

"I am Dr. Antonio Laguna; this is my wife, Consuela." A woman, similarly attired stepped into the room. "How do you feel?" asked Laguna in impeccable English. "You've had a bad time." I tried to nod. Every sinew and muscle in my body ached. "We've been looking after you for more than a week now. Your friend Dr. Orfila and another man brought you. You were badly injured." I tried to nod again. It wasn't happening. "How much do you remember, Lucy?"

eyes. I had absolutely no idea where I was or how I had got there. I had no concept of time, date or place. It was an extraordinary sensation, but not unpleasant. When I woke again, the room was dark.

I called out, "Hello." My voice sounded weak. Nobody came, not then, although I had the vaguest impression of my head being lifted off the pillow and water poured into my mouth, very gently. And then I couldn't stop the urge to drink more and more.

"Slowly, my child, slowly," a woman's voice, mellifluous and reassuring, speaking in Spanish. The next thing I knew, my head was back on the pillow and the woman had left, but a tang of her scent hung in the air. Of course, I was in Spain. But what had happened? Why was I here in this place, wherever it was? I tried to think. Was I sleeping or daydreaming? I had plenty of time to wonder because nobody bothered me for quite a while. Some unanswered questions came to mind. Why did Heinrich Müller kill that girl, Sophie Vidal? She was more or less my age. That was where it had all started, at La Maison Jaune in Arles.

WAITRESS SLAIN IN ARLES

I could see the newspaper headline in my mind, with the article and accompanying photograph. Why did Müller kill her? For money? No, surely not. A waitress wouldn't have had nearly enough cash for engine parts and fuel, more like pocket money for clothes and cigarettes. And what was it Villiers had said? – British Intelligence surmised that he had been heading west –

Laguna

Dr. Antonio Laguna's Surgery, Villaricos, Spain.

I OPENED MY EYES to see a ceiling fan rotating above me, and I immediately wondered about its number of revolutions per minute. It was just the sort of question my father would have asked himself, and the thought made me smile. The room I was lying in was painted white, its windows shuttered to reduce the intensity of the fierce Spanish sunlight.

The all-pervading smell of surgical spirit was familiar from my childhood; a GP's daughter knew all about waging war on bacteria. And so did a former nurse. I was in a narrow bed lying flat on my back – which I never did – with my legs pressed together and my arms by my side. The sheet had been tucked in securely to prevent me from moving. My chest felt tight, and my lips were dry, but I was neither hungry nor thirsty; neither hot nor cold. In a way I felt empty and content. I tried to move my head, and then my chest felt tighter as if my skin were being

"You think..."

Brim cut him off, "Villiers' theory is that Cordera was acting as a courier for The Falange Española and, consequently, the last of the Nazi elite. They'd never make it to the Nuremberg Trials. It's a pity we can't check that burned list of German surnames against the Nazis who are, so far, unaccounted for."

"Cordera was flying them to North Africa and freedom? Is that the contention?"

"Yes," agreed Brim, "but if the police captain in Villaricos – Alfredo – knew about the biplane and issued a licence ..."

"Then he also knew about the fugitive Nazis – or was a part of it?"

"Possibly," said Brim. He turned his attention from the nanny outside and focused it fully on Penfold. "The question is, does that affect Lucy? And Villiers too, for that matter. The sooner they are out of there, the better."

They were interrupted by a man's voice: "Your table, Professor."

Brim finished the last of his sherry and nodded, "Come on, John, let's try and forget about work for an hour." He took one last look out of the window at the scene in the Square. A pigeon had messed on the cabriolet hood of the pram. The nanny was frantically trying to sponge it off, and Brim suddenly laughed out loud.

Penfold turned, surprised: "Something amused you, Brim?"

"Yes, and I think they call it just deserts," and he followed

one fragment was a part of a list of typed German surnames. It was extremely delicate, but legible."

Penfold was intrigued: "Typed?"

Brim took a piece of paper from his suit pocket and started to read, "Yes, Villiers noted them. Krüger, Bauer and Louis Köhler; presumably not the German composer of the last century."

"And?"

Brim chuckled: "Don't you see? The use of the umlaut means the list was typed on a German-made typewriter like an Optima or Adler, which would suggest that it was an official document, possibly typed before the fall of the Third Reich." Brim sipped some sherry and looked at Penfold like a canny chess opponent.

"Which is why Müller had to destroy the list." Penfold said.

"Yes, he couldn't risk just tearing it up, or even flushing it down the lavatory. He had to make sure the evidence was destroyed. Villiers is onto something. Maybe our man had to leave in a hurry."

"So, who were these people?"

"Escapees from Germany, I would think. Senior Reich and so on. And with typical Nazi efficiency, the names weren't just scribbled on a bit of paper, they were typed, which means there could also be carbon copies in circulation. What Villiers couldn't determine is whether the flower-pot version was the original master copy typed by Müller or, more likely, by one of the secretaries at the Führerbunker. They had plenty of time."

"Good God, yes. Hitler was down there for weeks."

process of filling and lighting his notorious briar. Brim steepled his fingers and focused his gaze on a nanny outside who was feeding pigeons while her charge slept next to her in a large pram. He was quite convinced that this practice would one day bring about the end of the world, with pigeons and gulls the size of aircraft sweeping down from the sky to seize food uninvited. They would surely take over, if not prevented.

"Apparently, Lucy remembers the attack, and she remembers running, but very little else," said Brim. "She also remembers her friend Maria fainting in the kitchen. But she doesn't remember how she got there. According to Villiers, the evidence points to Lucy having been attacked upstairs in her bedroom. The local doctor is letting her convalesce in a small room above his surgery. His wife will nurse her. There is no hospital, and Lucy lost a lot of blood. She's tired and very confused. Poor girl."

"Amnesia?" suggested Penfold through a lunt of smoke.

"Shock, I would say, and blood loss: something no training in the world can prepare you for. And she is one of the best," said Brim as their sherries arrived. "Thank you, Wilkinson," said Brim, still watching the nanny.

"Professor," said the waiter, in a deferential tone.

"Something else Villiers said struck a chord. It may or not mean anything. After the doctor and police had left the Residencia, he made a thorough search of Müller's apartment next door. Every nook and cranny, as he put it."

"And?" asked Penfold.

*

Brim had chosen a private dining club in Bloomsbury for his lunch with Penfold – it was called The Literary Society, although few writers seemed to dine there. There was no sign outside the front door, which was permanently locked. The club's clientele included minor royalty, politicians, academics, senior medics and, of course, members of the Intelligence fraternity. The walls were covered with a dark red Chinese silk wallpaper. The Georgian windows of the restaurant were draped in rich fabrics and the floor was tiled with marble. The oak-panelled bar was obscured by clouds of tobacco smoke and busy with convivial chatter.

Brimblecombe and Penfold were shown to buttoned leather armchairs in the lounge overlooking Russell Square. Brim ordered Amontillado for both as an aperitif, to be followed by Salade Niçoise with a chilled Chablis. The Chef's highly recommended sirloin of roast beef would be washed down with a '36 Margaux, and the meal rounded off with port and Stilton. The two men silently thanked God for the fact that the meal was off-ration, and that the Club's legendary cellars had survived both the ravages of the Luftwaffe and the thirst of its convivial members.

"Excellent choice, Brim," said Penfold. "You wouldn't get anything like this in Berlin now. The buggers are obsessed with sauerkraut and onion. And steins of fizzy beer, of course. But you

measure, but for different reasons. It was a Friday, a little after noon; both men were dressed in civilian clothes and about to go out to lunch, but there was no urgency in Brim's demeanour.

"This Spanish doctor had to give her eight stitches? But she'll be all right? That's the main thing... understood," said Brim. "I'll notify Major Gubbins and Vera Atkins. They'll want to know."

He glanced across the desk at Penfold, who nodded. "Before you go, Villiers, I've spoken this morning to Henry Hobson at the British Consulate in Barcelona. Apparently, this Simon Avery character did leave his post unexpectedly. And Hobson did find part of a listening device concealed in his office: a microphone and some cable. So it is possible that his conversation with Lucy was overheard by Avery. Your man Dr. Orfila was right; there could have been some element of blackmail." Brim pursed his lips and listened to Villiers' response.

"Yes," he said, "that's true. But we need to know more about her attacker ... maybe she will be able to identify him in a day or so when she's up to it. But I'd like to get her out of Spain soonest."

Penfold mouthed the word 'Müller?' but Brim shook his head, as if to imply that this was not the time.

"The police in Bordeaux are conducting a thorough search of all likely establishments. All right, I'll speak to her tomorrow. Goodbye, Villiers. Oh, and well done." Brim replaced the receiver, sat back in his chair, lit a Senior Service with his familiar Ronson and reflected for a moment. "Lunch? I'll fill you

Penguin

British Intelligence Headquarters, London, England.

THE FOLLOWING DAY, the people of London were enjoying the hot summer weather. But it wasn't the intense heat of southern Spain that Lucy and Villiers were enduring at that moment. The offices of British Intelligence had their windows open and fans were working overtime to quell the heat. Secretaries wore summer dresses as they sat at their desks busy working on typewriters and telephones. BI were in contact with operatives all over the world, particularly Europe. This was the nerve centre of British Intelligence; a far cry from the romance of agents working abroad.

Professor Nicholas Brimblecombe was not a lover of summer; he abhorred personal discomfort of any sort. He sat at his desk, engrossed on the telephone. Colonel John Penfold sat opposite him, listening attentively and trying to deduce what he could from one side of the conversation. The information Miles

"For Lucy?"

"For both of us," said Villiers. Lucy's face flickered into a trace of a smile. And, at that moment, Villiers knew she'd be all right.

"Oh, Dr. Orfila?" Villiers asked.

The old man turned, "Si?"

"You are quite right. You'd better wake Captain Alfredo. There's a lot to be done. Christ, what a mess. Lucy's expression changed; she spoke very softly. Almost a whisper. Villiers had to lean down and put his face close to her to hear.

"Thank you ... Villiers."

He squeezed her wrist and whispered: "You – you are most welcome, Lucy."

And suddenly, Villiers realised that he had never felt more alive in his life. He would telephone Professor Brimblecombe in the morning with an update. He would want to know and so would Colonel Penfold.

suddenly shouted out in surprise.

“Oh yes, sorry. I neglected to mention that there’s a dead man over there. And his stiletto. My best guess is that he attacked Lucy with it. But why?” said Villiers. His tone was nonchalant.

“God knows what really happened here tonight.” Orfila shook his head. “Maria is not ready to speak of it.”

Lucy stirred again, and her eyes briefly flicked open. “Iodine ... cupboard.”

Orfila slapped his forehead with the heel of his hand. “Of course. The bottle you collected for little Ana.”

Orfila found the iodine, washed his hands meticulously and knelt beside Lucy.

“Let’s see what we have.” He carefully removed the cloths to reveal the flap of skin, then applied some iodine to the wound and replaced the flap of skin, irrigating the area with more iodine and speaking comfort to the patient. He was meticulous in his duty and spoke almost to himself:

“I can see it has stopped bleeding and the wound looks clean. But it will need a proper medical dressing. I have some at the pharmacy.”

“We can’t risk moving her,” said Villiers sharply. “Bring some bedding down, keep her warm. I’ll stay with her. And don’t forget the children.”

“I will go to them now.”

“Then get some dressings and bring them here – the keys are

Lucy and gently poured a trickle of water across the wound. The shock of it made her stir, which was a positive sign. He placed the cloths onto the wound and pressed down firmly to stem the bleeding.

"Compression," he said to reassure himself he was doing the right thing.

Lucy stirred again and tried to speak, "C–c–cold."

At that moment Orfila came into the kitchen. He was shocked at what he saw but impressed that Villiers had known what to do and had taken control of the situation so efficiently.

"Nasty cut across her chest," said Villiers looking up. "Knife wound. I've just cleaned it with cold water and I'm compressing it. It will need suturing, I'm sure. She's conscious but in shock. Pass those towels from over there on the ironing board and we'll wrap her up. Quick, we don't want her getting hypothermia."

They covered as much exposed skin as was practical. "You know what to do in an emergency, Villiers."

"First Aid training, plus a good deal of field experience. See if you can find some witch hazel or similar and check on the two children upstairs. They know you and it won't be such a shock for them if they wake up and see you." Villiers spoke with authority. He looked at Lucy's face and quickly checked her neck and radial pulses.

"Yes," said Orfila, "right away."

"How's Maria?"

"Asleep in the truck for now. She said some strange things.

Maria was rendered hysterical at the sight of her own home.

"I'll find Lucy. Christ! What's going on?" Villiers bellowed.

"Yes," said Orfila, "I'll stay with Maria until she calms down. She shouldn't be left alone."

The front door of the villa was wide open with the hallway and lounge area in total darkness. Villiers had an illuminated torch in one hand and his Walther in the other. Maria's bloody footprints showed him the way, but he had no idea what he would find. Once in the lounge he flicked the light switch and saw that the trail led down to the kitchen. Villiers continued cautiously down the tiled steps, flicked off the Walther's safety catch and listened with every nerve in his body on red alert. Training had taught him caution and patience, but he could smell blood, and spilled wine.

As he turned the corner into the kitchen's open entrance, he saw Lucy slumped on the floor with her back against a cupboard, apparently unconscious. The front of her blood-soaked nightdress was ripped open, exposing a massive horizontal cut across her chest which was still bleeding. He ran over to her, frantically calling her name, bent down to search for a neck pulse and listened for breath. Thank God, she was alive, just.

"Come on, let's get you lying down," he said to her. He grabbed a towel, rolled it to cushion her head and laid her flat on her back on the kitchen floor. He dashed over to the sink and filled a saucepan with water. He found clean cotton cloths in a drawer. There was a man's body on the other side of the counter,

Blood

Residencia López-Cordera, Villaricos, Spain.

MARIA STUMBLED CLUMSILY DOWN the road. Orfila and Villiers spotted her from the vehicle, the large bloodstains on her white nightdress showing up black in the moonlight.

"My God! Look, there's Maria," shouted Villiers, with uncharacteristic emotion. The truck screeched to a halt and both men jumped out. Maria was crying and shaking, with more blood on her hands, face and neck.

"Where's Lucy?" shouted Villiers desperately. "Where?"

Maria pointed at the residencia but was too traumatised to speak.

"Let's get her in the truck," said Villiers. "We can't waste a second."

They struggled to get her up and inside the front of the truck. Orfila sat with his arm around her. "Do you have a rug? She's freezing."

"There's a blanket in the back. It'll do. Nearly there."

pray you are unharmed."

The two men left the pharmacy, climbed into Villiers' truck and sped out of the plaza. Ten seconds after they'd left, Villiers' RT squawked back into life on Orfila's kitchen table: "Come in, Group Captain Villiers. SIB/NORTH/CRANWELL calling, come in please. Enter your usual caller recognition code ... come in, sir."

But Rosie Walker, the attractive RT operator with an enormous crush on Villiers, would be disappointed. Of course, she was keen to hear his voice, but she also had important news to convey to him. On the desk in front of her was an accident investigation report giving details of a biplane shot down in Tangier. A fireproof safe had been discovered at the crash site, and when opened it had been found to contain thousands of US dollars and a list of escaped Nazis.

The last name on the list was Heinrich Müller. Rosie bit her lip; she knew that name.

cleared out of his apartment in Barcelona. This suggests that he was, what, running away? But does anyone have any idea why?"

Orfila walked around, scratching his beard and mumbling to himself, "Could this Avery have been selling information to someone in Bordeaux about Lucy's visit to Barcelona? The portrait?"

"Wait a minute, Brim. Dr. Orfila has just raised a valid point."

Villiers explained to Brim what Orfila had just mooted and waited for his reply. "Maybe if you ask this Hobson character whether there is any chance their conversation could have been overheard by anyone. All right, Brim. Right away... yes, we'll go to her at the residencia right away. Goodbye for now."

Villiers rose from his seat: "Brim believes Lucy may be in danger. He is about to ring Jacques Labrut, the Police Commissioner in Bordeaux. He's a friend of Brim's and he knows Henry Hobson too, so he'll co-operate. No question of that. My God, Brim has contacts everywhere! He will ask for a team of gendarmes to be sent to every hotel, bar and restaurant in the city. They will ask whether any member of staff remembers seeing a disfigured British person meeting another man. If so, was there anything significant? An argument, for example. You know, Brim's hunches are usually right. He needs ID on that other person because it's probably Avery's killer.

Villiers opened his RAF rucksack, took out a Walther PPK, checked the clip and said, "Right, Residencia López-Cordera.

Pharmacy

Villaricos, Spain

MILES VILLIERS SAT AT Orfila's kitchen table surrounded by his RAF comms equipment. It was 3am and he was on the phone to Brimblecombe in London. He was urgently scribbling notes on his pad, and Orfila was at his shoulder hanging onto every word.

"You say the man was called Simon Avery. Murdered in Bordeaux, worked at the British Consulate in Barcelona; yes, Brim, I've got all that." The pad was covered in pencilled shorthand; Villiers wiped his brow.

"Where we went," whispered Orfila, "to send the cylinder."

Villiers waved his left hand irritably to tell him to be quiet; the old pharmacist looked offended. He also looked very worried. Villiers wrote down the name of Sir Henry A. Hobson, the Consul-General.

"Avery was killed by a stiletto. Punctured his liver and mesenteric artery – does Lucy need such vivid detail, Brim? –

comprehension dawning in them. I was convinced that I was a dead woman.

soaked dressing gown, collapsed to the ground in a heap. I scrambled over to her slumped body, exclaiming in Spanish which I hoped might sound convincing. I knelt at her side. I wondered if she had fainted on purpose.

"My poor sister!" I added some more solicitous words of Spanish, maintaining the charade. I could see Heller was now confused. He helped me get Maria upright. She was a dead weight. There was a lot of blood on the floor and I started to feel lightheaded.

"Why did you attack me," asked Heller very slowly, "if you are not Lucy Fry?"

I tried to shout at the stupid bastard, but I was weak and getting weaker by the second. "I defend me – myself."

Out of the corner of my eye, I could see Maria's empty wine bottle. It had rolled under a kitchen cupboard. It would be accessible as a weapon if I could distract Heller for long enough. I put my arm around Maria's shoulder, brushed the hair out of her face and kissed her forehead. I noticed she had blood all over her too. My blood. Her nightdress was soaked in it. I was now very lightheaded. I looked down at the wound, an eight-inch flap of skin hung open. I had lost a lot of blood. The room started to spin; my world was fading away.

"Mister – agua – water." I said and pointed at the sink.

Heller looked in that direction hesitantly and back at me and said: "Ja. Ok."

I saw him turn and thought briefly about making a grab for

muscle wound. Heller was dangerously quick. He spun around 180 degrees, his arm outstretched like a fencer, and the tip of his stiletto sliced across the front of my nightdress, tearing the material and slashing the skin above my breasts with a sweeping horizontal stroke from left to right. I felt my skin immediately split open. It stung like hell, but now he was facing almost away from me. Ignoring the pain, I attempted a commando-style palm strike and caught him on the jaw with the bridge of my hand, but it had little effect. He was too tall. I made a grab for the heel of the kitchen knife, which still protruded from his arm, but I missed, lost my balance and fell forwards. Damn! Too much Rioja earlier. I quickly looked down; my chest was bleeding badly now; I could feel the flow of warm blood running down to my stomach.

Maria stood frozen with fear, incomprehension and drink, watching the frenzied scene like a zombie. Heller came at me again like a boxer. He had pulled the knife out of his arm and there was no sign of the stiletto. His eyes were wild.

"Who are you?" I shouted, trying to sound Spanish, "Bandido!" My nightdress was soaked in blood and so was Heller's shirt.

"You are Lucy Fry?" he shouted. "British Intelligence."

"No. What is that?" I shook my head as if the idea was ridiculous.

For one short moment, a look of doubt crossed his face. He was expecting one woman and instead he got two. Not dissimilar

waited, listening. To my horror, Maria came into the kitchen, rubbed her eyes and went straight for a bottle of red wine, loosening the cork, upending it and taking a deep swig. She belched and swayed a little, clearly drunk, the bottle now empty.

"You killed my brother, you damned whore," the man screamed as he ran into the kitchen, with the stiletto in his hand. He was hysterical with rage, but he suddenly stopped, staring at Maria. Could this possibly be the wrong woman? His raised voice sounded German, and the penny dropped. Of course, this was Heller's brother. I had seen a framed family photograph at the house in Bordeaux. The two of them were not unalike, only a few years apart, and Dieter's weapon of choice had also been a stiletto.

Maria faltered, confused, but she didn't drop the bottle, fortunately. I gripped the knife and drew my arm back to throw it at Heller's neck, as I had been taught, then realised I didn't have enough space behind me to build up the momentum I'd need. If I stepped forward, I'd come out of the shadows and they'd both see me. I adjusted my grip – from the throwing position - until I was holding it like a dagger and ran at Heller side on. Ten feet of thrust propelled me toward his exposed jugular. I thought that I could easily kill him.

Heller and Maria both froze momentarily on seeing me. This time Maria did drop the bottle, which landed on her foot. She screamed, but the bottle didn't break. It just bounced and rolled away out of sight. The distraction caused Heller to move a

Soft footfalls, breath held, caution, stealth. These were the hallmarks of an assassin. I had known this night could come.

I gathered myself and quickly rolled further onto my left side. The figure now seemed suspended in mid-air holding the weapon in his right hand like a dagger. The thrust and power of his momentum drove him down into the net and frame. The blade plunged right through the mattress with such force it jammed into the wooden floorboard beneath.

A second later in one fluid movement I slid under the frame of the mosquito net, grabbed my little wooden bedside table by a leg, stood up and smashed it at the back of the man's head. He had moved, and it caught him on the shoulder instead, still trying to pull the blade from out of the floorboard, hampered by the netting and splintered wooden frame. I drove my bare heel down hard into the side of his head, catching the tip of his ear. He screamed out in pain but still struggled to retrieve the knife. He was broad shouldered and solidly built.

In theory I had a choice: stay to try and fight him or run, but this was obviously a premeditated attempt at murder, and the only sensible thing was to run. I took advantage of his momentary incapacity and raced out of the door. My assailant had known exactly where to find me and who I was. He intended to kill me and wouldn't leave until I was dead. As I ran, I glimpsed his face. Split-second. I knew I had seen it before. My mind was addled by sleep and panic, but this was precisely what I had been trained for.

genuinely shocked. The mere idea of a woman working abroad was a stretch for the generation of the Great War. By rights I should be married to a bank manager and living in Tunbridge Wells with two children: not working as a covert SOE agent in France and Spain.

How odd it would be to climb into a normal bed and not to have to lower the mosquito net with its rickety wooden frame and screws that always needed tightening. The residencia was deathly quiet as I lay in search of sleep, listening to the omnipresent sounds of crickets and distant dogs and, tonight, the strains of a Flamenco guitar not far away.

At least an hour must have passed when I heard my bedroom door being quietly opened. I had been dreading this moment. I hadn't had a chance to talk to Maria since it had become obvious that I was soon to leave Villaricos for the last time.

"Maria – please, we need to talk," I said softly into the darkness.

There was no response. No naked body slid in beside me. I opened my eyes and peered through the mosquito net, seeing nothing. Then I heard a faint whisper: it sounded like a blade being withdrawn from a leather sheath. Perhaps it was a stiletto? Every nerve in my body was now alert. Beaulieu training shot through my mind like a rapid film show: watch your back.

What to do: evaluate position: vulnerable, lying down naked and unarmed. My attacker – I had no doubt about his malicious intent – was standing with a weapon in his hand. Was it Müller,

Whisper

Residencia López-Cordera, Villaricos, Spain.

I WALKED BACK TO the residencia after 10 o'clock, sad at the prospect of leaving this pretty little village, but aware that I had no choice. With Müller almost certainly dead and rescue now easily available to me, the die was cast; I had no excuse. I assumed that HM Government was still paying me as it had been SOE's express instruction for me to remain in Spain.

It was beginning to get dark as I climbed the stone steps to my apartment. I put on my nightdress and washed in the tiny bathroom, staring at my face in the mirror as I dried it. The face reflected at me under the low wattage lightbulb was almost that of a stranger now. I looked older with my hair longer and my skin tanned by the sun. They won't recognise me in London, I thought with a smile. And what about my parents? My father, in particular. God, what was I going to tell him? He didn't even know what I really did for a living after East Grinstead. 'Oh, something for the MOD,' I had said vaguely when asked over

“Thank you. Absolutely nobody calls me Miles, I hate the name, so Villiers is still fine with me.” He grinned in a boyish way, and finally the ice was broken between us. Orfila smiled at this curious protocol that was so definitely English. I drank some wine and savoured the taste.

“But you didn’t catch Müller, as you had hoped,” I said finally. I emphasised the word catch as a euphemism for kill, and this wasn’t missed by Villiers who drained his glass with pleasure and grinned an even bigger grin.

“No,” he said slowly. “And, with luck, we won’t have to pursue any more Nazis on the run, in this part of the world. José is out of business for good.”

I smiled at Villiers – just to show him I could smile – and I was not always scowling: “Yes and that must be a good end to the story, finally.”

*

Orfila insisted on cooking a superb paella for us all, including Maria and the children. Antonio was mesmerised by Villiers’ radio equipment and was shown how to find radio stations from all over Europe. He was amazed at the sound of all the different languages – and music – and even the BBC External Service. Ana and Maria played board games quietly with me. It was a sad little gathering with the shadow of the accident hanging over us. Maria left early with the children, and I sensed that more was

Maria went to the school to fetch the children while I remained with Villiers and Orfila at the pharmacy. A bottle of Rioja was uncorked at six o'clock precisely, and we sat outside in Orfila's little courtyard. It was still warm and dry, and the air was infused with a delicious combination of fragrances: olive oil, garlic, lemons, fried fish and wine. I can only ever associate them with the southern Mediterranean. It was mouthwatering and magical, even when mixed with Spanish tobacco.Once away from his RT and relaxing, Villiers seemed to be a different person.

"This will change our plans, Miss Fry," he said as the three of us clinked our glasses. "We'll camp down here in Villaricos for another night, if that's all right with you, Dr. Orfila, and see if there are any further developments about the exact location of the crash site and the identities of the victims ..." He paused and looked at Orfila, who nodded in agreement ...

"It must be Müller and José. I am sure of that. We'll leave in the morning at first light. I'll radio the RAF aircrew at Murcia. I'm sure they won't mind a bit more time lounging around there. And thank you for what you told me about The Falange Española, Miss Fry. Interesting. We always thought that Spain would be Müller's springboard to his destination – but for you to be here as well – it was amazing, what you did with that portrait."

"Please call me Lucy," I said finally. "I think we can do away with the formalities, given the circumstances. Don't you?" The look on his face changed. He quaffed a generous mouthful of

"I have no information on the nationality of the perpetrators," said Villiers rather pompously. "I brought all this equipment in from my vehicle, to try and find out. I wanted to send an ETA signal to my people, but I was distracted. Air Traffic Control have reported nothing so far." He went on to say that he and Orfila had contacted the local police to report the family as missing, and that's how they had found out about the missing biplane.

Maria turned to me and said: "José and Henri ... dead?" She was the picture of tortured innocence. And I felt for her. I resolved to tell Villiers all about the conversation Maria and I had had about Henri, The Falange Española, how the operation had been financed and my conviction that Maria wasn't involved. Now was not the time – I went over to comfort her and explain as much as I could.

The day went on with Villiers sitting at the table, headphones clamped to his head, tuning from one radio frequency to another in search of further information about the plane crash. I made coffee and sandwiches while Orfila attended to the many patients and customers in the pharmacy. Many of them were probably wondering why there was an unknown vehicle parked right outside in the square. It had been commandeered by Villiers from ground staff at the seaplane training base in Murcia. Finally, at around four in the afternoon, Villiers announced that the aircraft had been identified as a Hawker Fury: a British-made biplane from the early thirties. People

“Let’s be clear about this, Miss Fry,” said Villiers. “Her brother helped Heinrich Müller evade justice. When did she tell you this?”

“Last night. Late. Too late to tell you.” My words came out too quickly. Did Villiers suspect I was hiding something?

“So when in God’s name did they turn up? And why wasn’t I told?” Villiers snapped. “Regardless of the time or inconvenience. Let’s have some answers, please.”

I said nothing.

Villiers continued, “I thought they were missing, in danger, and you couldn’t bear to leave until they were safely home. Wasn’t that the case? That’s why I agreed to stay on.” Sarcasm oozed from every word. And I really could not blame his attitude.

“What you say is true, Villiers. I was worried.”

There was a sudden crackling sound. The RT was whistling and popping with static and atmospheric interference. The voices which drifted in and out of audibility were talking fast in what sounded like Arabic. Mercifully, the interruption distracted Villiers from his line of questioning.

“Can’t understand a damned word of this gibberish,” he said irritably. “I’ll see if I can re-tune to another frequency.”

Captain Alfredo said something to Orfila and turned with his colleague to leave. Orfila said, “He apologises but has other police business nearby. He can come later but seeing as the crash happened outside Spanish territory it has nothing to do with him or his department.”

shortly afterwards, the aircraft took off. There was no mention of a destination. Or another passenger. Any thoughts, Maria?"

Maria shook her head and looked embarrassed; even though she couldn't have followed much of what Villiers had said, I am sure she got the gist. I couldn't imagine what was coming next. Villiers sat at Orfila's kitchen table, on which a radio transmitter had been set up with cables, headphones, microphone, and a Morse code transmitter. A length of wire connected the valve apparatus to a temporary aerial which must have been erected on the roof of the building. There was a page of handwritten notes and numerals, and an RAF chart of southern Spain and North Africa. It resembled an Ordnance Survey map, with one-inch square grid references and numerated air miles.

Villiers turned to Orfila, who had been standing quietly, and said, "Dr. Orfila, if you would please be kind enough to translate so Maria can understand this too. An RAF tracking station here..." he pointed at the chart, "has reported a downed aircraft 6 kilometres outside Tangier. It had flown from southern Spain. Some witnesses claim it was a biplane with no identification markings, and apparently no flight plan had been requested in either Spain or Morocco."

Orfila translated and I fancy he might have added a few other explanations about the nature of the comms apparatus on the table. I felt I needed to fill in a few blanks myself. Villiers was, as usual, carrying on like the counsel for the prosecution.

Alfredo and The Civil Guards

Pharmacy, Villaricos, Spain.

WE FOUND VILLIERS STANDING by Orfila's kitchen table with two civil guards dressed in full uniform. The table was littered with RAF communication equipment. “This is Captain Alfredo of the local police,” said Villiers, “and we have some news.” The second civil guard wasn't introduced. “It seems that the local police here did know that José Cordera was re-building a biplane, because he had to apply for a licence. Is that correct, Captain?” The man was a short, stout fellow with a bushy black moustache. He merely nodded his assent. Villiers' assumption that he spoke English was apparently correct. “It is also known that the biplane took off from an airfield near here yesterday. A large amount of aviation fuel was delivered to ...”

“San Felio,” put in Alfredo, with a twitch of his moustache. Groucho Marx, I thought, that's who he looks like. He was the spitting image; I couldn't get the thought out of my mind.

“Ah yes, San Felio,” Villiers agreed. It is understood the

she was totally unpredictable.

Then I heard the familiar sound of Orfila calling me, "Jovencita! Please come down!"

Quickly I shook off my slumber and donned my thin cotton dressing-gown. I padded barefoot down the stone steps outside the villa, to find Orfila pacing around and looking uncharacteristically anxious.

"Captain Alfredo of the Civil Guards needs to see you, Jovencita! Urgently." No niceties: I had never known him so fraught.

"Maria and the children are safe. They came home last night," I said quickly to assuage my guilt about not having rushed off to tell him in the early hours.

"I know, I have just seen them on their way to school." Orfila was perspiring with anxiety.

"So, what's the rush?" I asked hastily. "What's going on?" I tightened the belt of my dressing gown, feeling underdressed, and glanced around the street to reassure myself that none of the neighbours was about.

"Something has happened. You must come quickly. You and Maria. To the pharmacy."

At that moment, Maria turned the corner of the street and approached the villa. She carried a wicker basket containing a stick of bread, some vegetables, and a bottle of red wine, and looked her usual carefree self. She smiled at us both and said, "Good morning," a little self-consciously. I caught her eye, and her blank expression. There was no hint of the intimate moment

was pointless. I didn't turn around to see her and had no intention of encouraging her further. There was barely sufficient room for one on the single mattress: the mosquito net and frame were an encumbrance to movement. I heard Maria moan with sleepy pleasure and then her breaths became even and deep. There was a final whimper and, finally, she succumbed to sleep.

I knew I should have gone down the road to the pharmacy and told Villiers and Orfila the news about José, Henri and the biplane, but surely it could wait a few hours until morning? I was exhausted. And they'd ask questions I couldn't answer or didn't want to. They'd find out about Maria and the children soon enough anyway. Perhaps they'd ask her the questions and save me the trouble. Eventually I sank into glorious, untroubled oblivion. And I fancy I deserved it.

*

When I awoke the following morning, Maria was gone. I hadn't heard her go. I blinked as the daylight seeped into the room through the louvred shutters, lifted my head from the pillow and slumped back down again quickly. My head was a whirl. I knew I hadn't dreamt last night's encounter with Maria, and I could still smell her fragrance in my bed. And then I heard the usual racket downstairs that heralded the children's departure for school. The front door slammed shut and I automatically glanced at my watch. Damn. I had to get the news

expressions. “Usted y los niños?”

She sighed again sleepily: “Si Si. Si. Gracias ... Yes. We had to hide. Sorry.”

I wanted to ask her who’d written the note Orfila and I had found in the kitchen, but now was not the time. The words on the note were not true anyway and such a question would only alarm her. She snuggled in more closely. She couldn’t have manoeuvred herself any nearer to me. I swallowed; I needed some answers: “What happened to José?” I hoped that my question would motivate her to tell me what had become of Henri as well. Exactly where she and the children had fled to would come. In time.

She gripped me tightly: “José had a biplane and flew Henri to Tangier. I did not know this was going to happen before, I swear.” So that was what ‘Henri’ had wanted the money for: engine parts and fuel - for a biplane – that made sense. I stupidly hadn’t considered a biplane, only some kind of boat with a troublesome outboard motor.

“Why did José do it, Maria? Why did he risk his life? Tell me what you know, please.” I knew she would wait to compose her reply:

“José is member of - The Falange Española – the Spanish Fascist Party. Henri found him through friends in the party. He pay him much money. Muchas, muchas pesetas!”

She went on to say that José was a committed Fascist, so the flight to freedom wasn’t just about money. He believed the man

Safe

Residencia López-Cordera, Villaricos, Spain.

I WAS FAST ASLEEP in my makeshift bed, when Maria's semi-naked body slid under the mosquito net and bed sheet and lay quietly beside me. I was lying on my left side facing away from her. I always slept on my left side. Did she know that? I could feel her behind me, the weight of her breasts against my bare skin. I had sketched her; I knew the shape and every contour of her body. Her arm snaked around me. She squeezed me tightly, and I could smell her musky scent. There was a trace of perspiration, but it was not unpleasant. She was warm. She wriggled around like a small child trying to get herself comfortable. A thousand questions crossed my mind, but in the end the fact that she was here, and alive, was all that mattered at that moment. I broke the silence.

"Maria. Gracias a Dios. Estás a Salva? – Thank God. You are safe?" I said to her softly. All I could hear was a gentle sigh of confirmation. "And the children? Antonio and Ana, they are all

was bringing grains of sand into the cockpit. He could hear it slapping against the aircraft's fuselage and windscreen. The single engine started to misfire.

"We must land. There's the airport. Look at the oil temperature gauge." Cordera was desperate.

"No!" shouted Müller. "Not yet." Finally, freedom was near, he thought to himself. No Russians, no British, no Americans. And no trial. He thought of the French nanny's portrait in her sketch pad. He thought of her underwear on the line. There were plenty of women in Casablanca where he was going. He'd have his money, and Cordera's once he'd killed him. For a moment Müller closed his eyes and daydreamed, until he heard the noise.

It looked like lightning at first, or a giant firework. A massive shock of orange. And then the little Hawker Fury was no more. Fragments of flaming wreckage fell to the scorched earth like steel confetti.

clasped behind her neck, ample breasts, that haughty expression, her long black hair cascading down around her strong shoulders. Ah, now he understood. And he couldn't keep the smirk from his face. She was that kind of French nanny, the type he had heard rumours of: Parisiennes with a penchant for...

"I'm looking at the co-ordinates for our destination." Cordera broke into his fantasy. "We're heading 35* 46' North, 5*48' West. Tangier – Boukhalef airport. About five minutes." Cordera's right hand moved toward the radio transmitter. He was about to flick the switch. From behind Müller could see him move.

"No radio," said Müller, "absolutely not."

"But we have to alert the authorities in Tangier. They must tell us where to land. Weather conditions on the ground, wind speed. This is not an emergency."

"No radio," he said again. He produced a Luger from a holster inside his jacket and laid it on his lap. He would shoot him through the back of his pilot's seat if he had to.

Had they had their radio switched on, they would have heard the ground operator say, "If you do not identify yourself, we will shoot you down. You will be considered as an enemy to this country."

Cordera was really sweating now because he knew the standard international aviation regulations. There was a lot of sand between Tangier in the north-west and Tétouan in the east, near the Mediterranean. Cordera couldn't risk putting down in

to gauge if he was serious. His belt restricted him.

"So what?" said Cordera simply. He stared out through the cockpit window at the swirling clouds in front of them. His eyes flicked to the instrument panel again.

"Did she tell you any..." Müller was suddenly craving information. He wanted salacious details, confidences broken and secrets revealed, "... any details at all?"

"No." Cordera looked from port to starboard. There was a touch of turbulence from the rising heat, and the old plane shuddered. He was gripping the stick for dear life, which he shouldn't be doing. 'A lightness of touch.' Olivares had taught him 'Feel the plane. See what she wants and respond. Like being with a woman!' He had laughed.

They were entering Moroccan airspace now; it was a very short distance from the Spanish mainland to the tip of North Africa at Punta de la Almina. Had their radio been turned on, they would have heard the ground operator say, "Unidentified aircraft, come in. Please identity yourself. There is no record of a flight plan lodged with us. Please come in. Urgent."

"The children adored her," continued Cordera. He was getting twitchy.

"Screw what the children thought of her," said Müller, licking his thin, bloodless lips. He wanted details about Maria and the French nanny whose silk underwear he had caressed as it dried on the washing line at the villa, whose room he had searched and whose sketch pad he had flicked through when she was out

with a vague smell of fuel. Cordera and Müller communicated via headphones – on the internal radio - in broken Spanish because the former had no German or English.

"What did you make of my neighbour at your residencia, José?" asked Heinrich Müller. The question came out of the blue and startled Cordera. For a moment, Cordera's mind flashed back to the wonderful, carefree evenings he had had with Maria and the children and their new houseguest, the beautiful Claude Moreau from Paris. He had had reservations about her actual identity, but she was pretty, with high cheekbones and blue eyes. He had seen through her dowdy local clothes and lack of makeup to the sensual beauty beneath, assuming that she was making a deliberate attempt to go unnoticed. He had begun to regret the days he spent away from the villa, fixing the engine in a tiny workshop near Villaricos with Müller occasionally helping and Captain Alfredo watching over him. Fishing? God, he hadn't been fishing for weeks.

"I think my sister is in love with her," said Cordera candidly, "and I don't blame her. She's gorgeous, and what a beautiful figure! I have seen her swimming in a secluded cove near Villaricos. Just her underwear. She has the body and poise of an athlete."

Despite his murderous past, Müller was still capable of being shocked. "In love with her?"

"Yes. I used to watch Maria looking at her."

"But she was married. Mein Gott! She has children!" said the

José

Strait of Gibraltar, Spanish Airspace.

JOSÉ CORDERA CHECKED HIS gauges and instruments as his flying instructor, Captain Manuel Olivares, had taught him all those years ago. Altimeter, air-speed indicator, altitude-indicator, climb and descent indicator, oil pressure and temperature gauges. He was hot under the collar; his passenger in the seat behind him could not see his anxiety. But he could certainly hear it.

Cordera scrutinized the directional gyro and compass to confirm the bearing. On his lap lay a section of folded chart with his course carefully plotted and timed on it in pencil. The plane's radio was switched off because his flight was neither authorised nor known by air traffic control in either Spain or Morocco, but radio silence had a price for many practical reasons.

They were flying a Hawker Fury, a battered British biplane built in 1931. The Rolls-Royce 12-cylinder Kestrel engine chugged on relentlessly. The cockpit of the single-propeller

there. The danger is now in North Africa. Not here in Villaricos. This, I think, makes sense."

God, how I wanted to smile, to laugh, rejoice. But I knew I must remain stoical, not show my feelings.

"Very well," said Villiers finally, "but only for twenty-four hours. And the clock is ticking." He looked at me again. "Sorry I had to be so firm on this, Miss Fry." I said nothing, nodding again to acknowledge his apology.

Orfila stood and looked at me, equally stoical. "A glass of wine, Jovencita?" Then his brown eyes shone, and his leathery old face creased into a smile. Was I that easy to read? I must be getting rusty.

Villiers looked at Orfila and then at me, saying nothing. Orfila didn't move, but I could feel him willing me to back down. I couldn't. "Well then, let's just guess, shall we? Find Müller, kill him. And bring me out. Never mind the consequences."

Villiers huffed:

"In a nutshell, yes. The Cordera family – Maria and the children at least – are innocent bystanders in the wrong place at the wrong time. It's unfortunate, but there it is. If Müller is a hopeless cause, then so be it. Plan B: find Lucy Fry, pull her out and take her back to London. May I remind you, Ensign Fry, that you have responsibilities under the Official Secrets Act. As an agent, you have classified knowledge of SOE and MI6 ops abroad."

"I was their agent abroad during the war," I snapped, "which I understand is now over."

"Let me make this perfectly clear, Miss Fry, you are still Brim's agent in Europe until he signs you off. And not before. Do you understand?"

I nodded, alarmed. His tone was adamant. He didn't shout. He didn't have to. Villiers had an authority which filled the room. A public-school lawyer making a closing statement.

Orfila said, "Why don't you wait for forty-eight hours, Group Captain Villiers? If José Cordera does come back, and I think he will as he has nowhere else to go, he can tell Lucy where Maria and the children are and tell you the fate of the Nazi." The cool kitchen fell silent for a moment as we all wrestled with our

"Don't you think they should stand trial?" I couldn't help asking, just to get an idea of his opinion.

Villiers dabbed his face again. "They should stand in front of a firing squad. That's my view, plain and simple, but there we are." I nursed a tumbler of water. The three of us sat around Orfila's olive-stained kitchen table like distraught relatives in a hospital waiting room. Villiers re-folded his map and looked at me.

"Sorry to rant, but there we are. I've seen enough of it." He paused. "Listen, there's an RAF Lysander at the training base at Murcia - the one I came in on – it's waiting to take you back to England. Brimblecombe's orders. He wants a full de-brief on how you escaped from France with the help of the Resistance. Major Pelham from Poundon was impressed with your clever use of the poem code from Tarbes. That RO in Tarbes obviously knew what he was doing: two minutes and three seconds!"

How much did Villiers know? The atmosphere was awkward because I had no intention of going anywhere. Not yet. And when I did it would be on my terms. Not his. I took a breath and faced him: "I am not going anywhere until we find Maria and the children. I am responsible for them."

"No, you are not responsible for them, Miss Fry." Villiers raised his voice like a courtroom barrister. "What happened here was pre-planned. Müller contacts Cordera – how or why is still unclear – who hides him and then helps him escape to North Africa. He is a wanted war criminal, and my orders are clear."

I looked at Villiers and saw a bead of perspiration on his forehead. I asked him, "How did Müller escape from Germany?" It was a question that had been on my mind. I had images of sealed borders and British troops marching beside barbed wire fences.

Villiers eyed us both as if deciding how much he could reveal. "Ever heard of Ratlines?" We both nodded our heads. I certainly had, and I had told Orfila all about my escape from France. Villiers took out a handkerchief and mopped his brow. "Do you have any idea how many Nazis have escaped and evaded capture?" This time we both shook our heads. How could we know? It seemed we were a long way from Germany. "The answer is in the thousands." He continued: "Ratlines are a complex system of escape routes for Nazis to flee from the Fatherland to a safe haven. Their destinations are often in South America: Argentina, Paraguay, Colombia, Brazil, Uruguay and Mexico."

Orfila shrugged, "But how do they leave Germany?"

"Through Austria or Italy," said Villiers. "There are always people willing to help them for enough cash. The escapees buy disguises and false papers. The four we are keenest to capture are Adolph Eichmann, Josef Mengele, Klaus Barbie and -"

"Heinrich Müller," I put in quickly. "And there are others according to the phone call I overheard."

"Exactly. Monsters, all of them. All responsible for unspeakable atrocities against mankind. They should be made to

unearthed one of the most wanted men in the world. He killed Sophie Vidal, robbed the hotel's cash register and fled with the money. The man is a psychotic killer." Villiers went on to say that British Intelligence surmised that Müller had been heading west from Montpelier to Perpignan, Barcelona and then Villaricos. My portrait of Henri, he said, had been very useful and had prompted Villiers's mission to Spain. He wasn't just there to evacuate me; he was also there to find Müller.

"But why here?" said Orfila. "Why did he come to Villaricos?"

Villiers sniffed. "More specifically, how did Müller know that José Cordera would shelter him? Would his sister have known?"

"No," I said firmly, "Maria may be naïve, but she is a devoted mother with protective instincts. I would bet my life that she would never do anything to put her children in harm's way."

Villiers continued, "If Cordera has transported Müller to a Spanish port like Tarifa, for example..." He took a map of Spain from his jacket pocket and spread it out on the kitchen table, as Orfila had done before him. "It is likely he will cross the Strait of Gibraltar to Morocco – Tangier perhaps. Once he is in North Africa, he can travel south to Casablanca. We'd never find him. Not a chance."

"I see," I said.

"The point is," Villiers went on to say, "José Cordera will have to come back to Villaricos."

"Why? He and Maria are brother and sister, not husband and wife, and the children are his niece and nephew."

and I had made the journey to the British Consulate in Barcelona, my discussion with the Consul-General, and my wish to get the cylinder containing the sketched portrait to Brimblecombe. Now was not the time to mention my mission in Bordeaux.

Orfila added the odd embellishment to add credence and authenticity to my tale, and finally, he handed Villiers the crumpled copy of Le Figaro with its stark headline:

WAITRESS SLAIN IN ARLES.

Villiers had only uttered one word – Müller - during my long monologue. He listened intently without taking notes, as if he were filling in the pieces of a mental jigsaw. Concentration was written on his face as I completed the story.

"Thank you, Miss Fry. Let me tell you what we know. You might have some ideas. A few eyewitnesses stated that Müller fled from Berlin on 1st May, the day after Hitler committed suicide. We believe he may have found a haven in Italy for a few months, but that is purely conjecture." Villiers looked away from me for a moment. "It is our belief that he took a ferry from Italy to Corsica and then travelled on to Marseille. An SOE agent was certainly killed by Müller, but not before a detailed report had been filed to an MI6 agent in Paris. And then a telegram sent to London. The agent also stated that he believed Müller had killed a girl called Sophie Vidal." He picked up the newspaper. "So that confirms precisely the story in this article."

"And the photograph," I put in. "That's him. Henri is

overwhelming. And I wondered, deep down, if there was a sense of jealousy. It was me, after all, who had raised the alarm in the first place: by sending the drawing – via the Consulate – direct to Brim. I bit my lip and decided to simply play the game. He needed to know the whole story if things were to progress in a civilized manner. I turned to Villiers and composed myself. Orfila could see what was going on in my mind and I detected a very slight smile as I explained.

I told Villiers my Spanish story from the beginning: how I had found Residencia López-Cordera through an advertisement in the local shop and been 'interviewed' by José, Maria, Antonio and Ana. I described how my role as a tenant had evolved into becoming a nanny to the children and kitchen help for Maria in lieu of rent. I told him about our family games with drawings and words. Villiers listened intently. I described the man we all knew as Henri. His surreptitious arrival and how I had overheard his telephone conversation at the post office, his urgent need for money to buy engine parts and fuel; the mention of the Banco Etcheverria and finally the exchange of American dollars for pesetas ...

Then I took a deep breath and repeated what he had said about me: Someone else is staying at the Residencia. A woman, on her own... She must be a spy. Maybe ex-Resistance? I should kill her, but I can't take the risk of being caught and arrested. I have to get out of Spain and there are others coming.

Villiers looked highly alarmed and said almost to himself.

have travelled a long way, by air and land, and I want answers. Do you understand me?" His tone was firm; he clearly meant it; and Villiers could see that he had taken the wind out of my flimsy sails.

"Come back to the pharmacy," said Orfila, ever the mediator. "I can close early. The villa is too far. And here is too public." He glanced over at his premises, which could be clearly seen from the main square. Villiers nodded his agreement and we started to walk.

"Actually, I have no idea where he is," I said clearly. "Henri – the name I knew him by – has vanished."

"Quieter," said Villiers sharply. He shot me a look.

I lowered my voice: "The Spanish family I am staying with has also vanished." I knew I was being petulant, but I couldn't help it. And I couldn't understand why Brim had sent such an envoy as Miles Villiers. Brim must have known that I would dislike him, and I was still miffed about the 'moth' betrayal.

As we reached the exterior of the pharmacy, Villiers's face broke into a charming smile. It was almost as if he had read my mind – perhaps he had. "All the more reason why we need to talk, Miss Fry. I am sorry if I was abrupt, but you can see the urgency of my mission here. And thank you, Dr. Orfila, for your kind offer of sanctuary. Your contribution to the conversation would be of value too, so I hope you will join us."

The freckled face creased into a smile and Orfila muttered something about 'my pleasure', as we entered the cool building.

hated being made to feel like a damsel in distress rather than how I perceived myself: an undercover agent awaiting orders from British Intelligence in London.

"Dr. Mathieu Orfila," Orfila said meekly. Humility and good manners prevented him from expanding on his crucial role as pharmacist and medical adviser to the local community, particularly the poor and elderly. And young children like Ana.

"Can we go somewhere to talk, Miss Fry?" Villiers said again, with just a hint of impatience. He looked at Orfila appealingly, as if hoping he might help him with this uncooperative female.

Orfila was about to speak, but I placed my hand on his bare forearm to stop him. Villiers watched this somewhat intimate gesture with confusion. He was probably speculating about the nature of our relationship. It was a palpably father-and-daughter dynamic now; or at least something in the order of uncle and niece. "I don't want to be evacuated," I persisted.

Villiers took a breath and lowered his voice: "The drawing – which you obviously went to a great deal of trouble to send to the Professor in London via the diplomatic bag – was of Heinrich Müller, head of the Gestapo. He is one of the most wanted Nazis in the world, responsible for mass murder."

This time we all took a breath.

"I told you I had seen that face," said Orfila, without thinking. I could have strangled him for encouraging Villiers so readily. I didn't want to give him any more information than I had to. Not yet at least.

wrong foot. I cursed Brim inwardly.

He lowered his voice. "Evacuation. I've come to take you home. Your mission is accomplished." A trace of a smile creased his freckled face.

"Do you have identification, Mr. Villiers?" My abrasive tone took him aback. He quickly delved into his air force-style jacket pocket, retrieved his British passport and an RAF/SIB/North/Cranwell ID card and held them out for my inspection. I gave them a cursory glance and nodded, like an indifferent border guard, not at all as if I were anxious to go home.

"Scorpius – the Artist," he said, as if revealing the fact that he knew my call sign might encourage me.

"I don't want to be evacuated," I said abruptly. Villiers was taken aback once more. I gave him the scowl I reserved for my father. The one I had used so much growing up in Devon.

"Is everything all right, Jovencita?" Orfila appeared out of nowhere, blinking in the bright sunlight which filled the busy square. He was wearing a long white lab coat with short sleeves and a circular neck. He must have been watching me from his pharmacy window. He often did; he was fiercely protective, particularly since the Cordera family had disappeared.

"Yes, thank you. This is Mr. Villiers. Apparently, he wants to evacuate me." There was more than a trace of sarcasm in my voice. I found Villiers' manner contemptuous.

Villiers thrust out a large hand. "Group Captain Miles

into Plaza de la Constitución, and there was Villiers, sitting in the shade of a tree on a low brick wall outside the church. He stood and walked towards me. Then he seemed to alter his direction, albeit very slightly. It was all part of a play for my attention, which was annoyingly successful.

"Papillon de nuit, Mademoiselle?" he said, not looking at me, in fact, looking in the other direction completely. Moth! I knew what had happened at once, of course. He was one of Brim's men and Brim had disclosed my alleged phobia. A family joke initiated by my father years ago. At this moment it felt like a betrayal, and Villiers thought he was being frightfully clever using such intimate personal knowledge as a make-do password. I was furious. He stuck out like a sore thumb among the crowd of Spanish locals, and just those few words revealed that his accent was appalling. Calling it schoolboy French would be an insult to schoolboys.

"What?" I asked, turning slightly to face him and careful not to be overheard. I had altered my appearance considerably since my service file photo had been taken. I was dressed in a Mediterranean-style black shawl, my head and shoulders covered, like widowed women. I assumed I'd melted inconspicuously into the local scene and looked the part. I was irritated that Villiers had recognised me so readily. My attempt hadn't fooled this particular man, with his warped sense of humour about recognition codes.

"Miles Villiers," he said disarmingly. "Sorry, I thought you'd

Papillon

Plaza de la Constitución, Villaricos, Spain.

AS SOON AS I SAW Miles Villiers, I knew he'd be troublesome. I sensed it from something in his eyes: conceit. And later from the way he walked off with annoying self-assurance. It wasn't quite a swagger, more an ebullience. Whereas Freddie was self-deprecating and reserved, this man possessed, or seemed to possess, extraordinary vanity. He was a sportsman, certainly, possibly a boxer or a rower. He was of average height with sandy-coloured hair and was unmistakably the product of an English public school. I could see that he would be attractive to a lot of women. Nothing in the world could have prepared me for what he said by way of introduction, and that irked me even more.

I had just left Orfila's kitchen after morning coffee and pastries he had made from almonds, beaten eggs and ground cinnamon. They were delicious when dunked into the strong, black coffee he had brewed. He had read me the newspaper in

Avery finally slumped to the marble floor; his chin cracked onto the edge of the basin. His last thoughts were of Salisbury Plain, a military exercise in the rain and mist. Sergeant Hughes suddenly shouting: "Be careful, men. This place is mined, watch where you step..."

As he lay dying, he translated Heller's words in his mind and closed his eyes: I had a feeling I might get my money back, Herr Avery ...

kidney, puncturing his mesenteric artery and other internal organs, He twisted it brutally and then withdrew it in one movement. Avery grunted in disbelief. The water in the sink changed from the colour of diluted coffee to red, as blood spewed from his mouth and the brutal wound. The water was now the colour of rust. For a moment, Avery caught sight in the mirror of the German behind him in his expensive suit and fedora. Avery just could not believe that his life would end like this. He had dreamed of a comfortable retirement, living off the money on the French Riviera.

"Goodbye, Avery." Heller wiped the bloody stiletto onto Avery's crisp white shirt, splitting the skin on his back as he did so – he was losing blood rapidly now. Heller found Avery's jacket folded neatly on a wooden bench. He removed the envelope and placed it back in his own pocket. Then he found the leather notebook and quickly flicked through the pages to find lines of notes written in English about Lucy Fry: detail after detail from the conversation Avery had overheard between Hobson and her at the Consulate.

Then a few words captured his attention because they were underlined: tiny room... young family... Villaricos ... Heller smiled to himself, tapped the rim of his elegant hat and addressed a few last words in German to the bleeding man. Then he turned and walked away, briefly checking his own clothes for bloodstains. All he could think of was killing Lucy Fry in the same way. He gritted his teeth, his jaw muscles taut with anger:

behind. Heller slackened his pace, anxious for more information. "This Lucy Fry. Where does she live?" He lit a cigarette.

"I don't have her address."

"Really?"

"No. But she came to the British Consulate in Barcelona. So, Spain." Avery sounded shaky, unconfident; Heller could tell that he was lying.

"Spain is a big country. Can you find out?"

"I can't go back to the Consulate. Not now. This money is my escape plan." He touched the plump envelope in his pocket.

They approached the entrance to the railway station. Avery faltered: "I must try and get these coffee stains out of my suit. It's new. But I think our business is concluded, so, I'll say goodbye, Mr. Heller." There was no handshake. Avery hobbled off towards the railway station cloakroom.

"Ja," said Heller softly. "Goodbye." He looked at the station clock and then at his watch, as if checking its accuracy. He also walked in the direction of the cloakroom, stretching a pair of tight leather gloves over his fingers. He glanced left and right, as a precaution.

Simon Avery was standing at a basin in a booth in the cloakroom toilets, in his shirt and underclothes, sponging the stains with a water-soaked handkerchief, his tin leg visible. He turned as Heller approached.

"Oh, it's you! It's worse than I thought. Bloody black coffee!"

Heller checked his surroundings and discreetly withdrew a

"I am very aware of my brother's achievements," Heller said quietly and very deliberately. "Dieter was a naval hero, an asset to Admiral Dönitz and the Kriegsmarine. And now he is dead. That bitch killed him – and she'll die for it."

A flurry of waiters and waitresses came hurrying over to clean up the mess with buckets, sponges and plenty of fuss. Avery laughed, seemingly oblivious to the commotion. "At least he went out in style. God, but she was an absolute beauty. I did see her, of course. Dark hair, blue eyes and very curvy." He was still reading the notebook. A dirty grin crossed his twisted face. He was almost salivating at the thought of Lucy. She was the probably the most beautiful woman he had ever seen. And he remembered every detail of her.

"What do you mean?" Heller asked slowly as the clean-up progressed, more discreetly now.

Avery continued: "Stunning is the word. And her orders were obviously very clear," he said crudely: "'Find Heller. Fuck him. Finish him.' And she did. He fell for her, like a fool."

That was enough. Heller was humiliated. The memory of his dead brother was being demolished by this crippled English traitor with his tale of an English tart. But he quashed his anger. "Please leave us," Heller said with authority. "This is a private matter. A bereavement." The embarrassed staff crept away from the awkward scene with bowed heads.

"Come on," said Avery. He picked up the toppled tray and placed some money on it. "I think we should leave now anyway. I

"I see."

"She works for Professor Brimblecombe, head of British Intelligence. My – er – former employer, Sir Henry Hobson, knows this man, from diplomatic circles, I expect."

Heller was surprised. "British Intelligence, eh? Interesting."

Avery continued: "Yes, I thought so. Her orders, it seemed, were simple. Find the U-Boat Commander who is responsible for sinking the most substantial tonnage of Allied shipping. Find him and kill him."

"I see," Heller said again. He couldn't believe the unvarnished truth. He had been told a quite different story of patriotic heroism. Had his brother really been duped by a beautiful woman? And a British spy at that? Was it possible? Heller continued, partly curious, mainly ashamed. "What was she like, this Lucy Fry? Did you see her?"

Avery nodded. He was keen to move on, but a trace of something like a smile crossed his face. It was fleeting, but it was there. He turned a page of his notebook, "Commander Dieter Heller had quite a record. Let me see now: 34 ships sunk and God knows how many Allied sailors and supplies lost in the Atlantic. Oberkommando der Marine should have awarded him the highest honour; instead they invented a fairytale that he was killed in action at sea. Ha!"

Heller shot out of his chair, his cup and saucer went flying, coffee splattered up the wall and over Avery's suit. The tray dropped down to the carpeted floor. He quickly regained his

his family in Germany.

"So, what do you have for me? Your telephone call had us intrigued. And my family alarmed." Karl Heller sat forward as the waiter discreetly delivered the coffee and poured two cups carefully. The waiter placed the bill on the tray. He waited and when it was apparent he was not going to get paid yet, moved away.

"Her name is Lucy Fry. She is certainly the spy who killed your brother. I heard it with my own ears at the Consulate. I'd quickly wired in the listening device, the moment I knew there was a woman with French ID at the gatehouse. She looked like trouble and I sensed an opportunity to make money. I was right, of course. I briefly thought she might have suspected me, but I doubt it. I was too clever for her."

Heller looked perplexed, almost disappointed and he repeated her name to make sure he had heard it correctly: "But you told me on the telephone her name was Claude – something – from the French Resistance." He ground his teeth as he spoke the last two words. "Not Lucy Fry."

"I did, and a lot of people probably believed that name too," said Avery. "She played the part well and fooled many. She is clearly an actress." Avery took out a leather notebook and consulted its long, thin pages. He held it close to his eyes, almost as if he were too vain to wear glasses, or more likely couldn't afford them, yet. Heller picked up a cup and saucer and delicately sipped his coffee. He winced; it was strong and hot.

"Let's go into the hotel," said Heller. "I need coffee."

They wandered towards the entrance. The head porter held the door open for them to pass. Heller noticed Avery had a pronounced limp and wondered what accident had caused such facial and physical disability. An air crash? Maybe he was ex-RAF. But he wouldn't ask; they were there for a business transaction and that was that. And yet, he was still curious. They settled in the corner of an alcove at the rear of the downstairs lounge and Avery ordered coffee in excellent French from a passing waiter. The waiter paused and waited for Heller's order.

"And for me too, black coffee, please," said Heller in perfect English. He continued, "My family and colleagues were curious when we received the telegram about Commander Heller, my brother. The information is genuine? Because, if not..." His words trailed off, leaving a slipstream of menace.

Avery's tongue flicked out of his mouth like a lizard's. "Yes, it's genuine, and checkable. But I need to see the money, I have risked a lot to come here."

Heller put his hand into his left jacket pocket and pulled out an envelope with bank notes protruding from its aperture as if stuffed in quickly. "There's enough in there to buy an apartment in Berlin."

"I don't want to buy an apartment, Herr Heller," Avery replied sharply, "and certainly not in Berlin. I hear the place is in ruins, and now the Russians are there, it must be even worse." The unfortunate choice of words came out distorted, and Heller

liveried head porter in a green uniform with gold buttons stood outside, his hands clasped in front of him, his eyes darting left and right; this was a superior establishment. A party of young ladies emerged from reception, dressed perhaps for a wedding, giggling, animated and clearly giddy with excitement. A concierge followed them, wearily pushing a squeaky luggage trolley on unsteady wheels. It was loaded with suitcases, dress carriers and bouquets of flowers. The head porter signalled to a nearby taxi, its engine idling while the driver read a newspaper. The girls bundled into the rear of the vehicle, seemingly oblivious both to the fate of their luggage and the matter of the fare.

Heller watched them with interest, and one caught his eye: auburn-haired, pretty, cotton dress and bare shoulders. She smiled at him fleetingly – sensing his appreciative gaze – and he nodded back courteously. Seventeen, if she was a day, not much older than his own daughter. He sighed. My God, and they're all so pretty, just like the German girls before the war. Ah! The 1930s in Berlin were his heydays.

Simon Avery, the unfortunate man from the Embassy in Barcelona, approached him awkwardly as the girls' bags were loaded into the boot of the taxi and its front footwell. Avery's hollow face looked pale, his eyes tired and bloodshot. One of the girls poked some francs out of the window of the taxi towards the concierge. An ample tip, thought Heller.

"I take it you have my money?" Avery said, greedily and

Heller

Quai Louis XVIII, Bordeaux, France.

KARL HELLER WALKED PURPOSEFULLY along Quai Louis XVIII, a wide promenade beside the river Garonne. Today it was turbulent and swelling over the banks. It was mid-July, late morning, and Bordeaux was quiet, the odd person wandering through the empty squares. He turned left into the rue Esprit des Lois. He wore expensive civilian clothes, was in his late thirties and quite dashing in appearance. The obligatory fedora gave him a stylish bearing; people might have thought he was a travelling salesman.

He clutched his left upper thorax area with his right hand, as if checking his heart was still beating. Heller looked anxious and preoccupied. He stopped outside the majestic-looking Hôtel de Normandie, which was set back in a grand, apparently affluent square. He glanced at his watch and lit a cigarette. A clock chimed eleven. With Teutonic punctuality he started walking. The arrangement had been to meet just after eleven.

Orfila shrugged; he too looked tired. "I doubt Maria can even write. It was intended for us to believe it was her."

"José?" I asked, examining it more closely. I knew the answer to that too.

Orfila cautiously sipped some of his wine and made a face: "No, surely not he."

"Then Henri wrote it," I said. I closed my eyes again. In all the parlour games we had played with drawings and words, I had never seen Maria write – only the children tried.

"So," I said firmly, "Perhaps José is helping Henri to escape to God knows where. Is that a possibility, do you think?"

"Maybe. Maybe not. But it still begs the question: where are Maria and the children?" Orfila's eyes glistened. He finished his wine and put his glass in the sink.

"Hidden somewhere. But where?" My brain considered a few possibilities.

"Let's pray neither José nor Henri has done anything stupid. Or God help me," said Orfila with surprising vehemence.

I gripped his arm; there was nothing to say. But I realised I would soon find out just how good a spy I really was.

I was soon to be tested as never before.

huge old Spanish wardrobe – the same. I glanced into the bathroom – nothing. I picked up the wastepaper basket, gave it a sniff. You never know. It was empty and dry.

"Where can they be?" asked Orfila. He had checked the other three bedrooms while I had conducted my search.

I ran down the stairs to the main family room where we had sung and played the drawing game. I thought of Maria and the children, and of José, the man who had arranged for Henri to live at the villa. My head swirled. I felt exhausted from travelling and I needed a drink. I walked down to the cool of the basement kitchen and found the usual bottle of red wine on the sideboard. I picked it up, and underneath it was a square of folded paper. Orfila picked the paper up as I poured two full tumblers of the deep red, viscous fluid. He unfolded the message and read it quietly.

"He has them, Jovencita," said Orfila. "The German has them."

I sank half the wine in one go, closed my eyes and thought of Brim and Freddie at the Savoy saying I would make the perfect spy. The wine tasted warm and sour as it had done in my dream on the boat.

The German has them. In that instant I knew it wasn't true. Why would a Nazi war criminal on the run risk kidnapping a woman and her two children? The note had to be a clever distraction.

"Whose writing is that?" I asked Orfila and realised that it

Message

Residencia López-Cordera, Villaricos, Spain.

SOMETIMES, WHEN THINGS APPEAR normal, you know they are not. Nothing was obvious, but as Orfila and I approached the Residencia, we both sensed instinctively that something was wrong. It had an unnatural stillness, like a vacant house. I glanced at my watch: it was nine-thirty in the evening and still light. Another hot July day was coming to an end. Orfila knocked on the front door and we waited. No noisy and excited children's voices sounded from within, no familiar clatter of pots and pans. The routine hubbub of domesticity was eerily absent. Something was definitely wrong.

I walked to the side of the villa and mounted the stone steps two at a time to my little apartment. Orfila followed. It was exactly as I had left it. All my possessions were in place – my camera, sketch pad and pencils. I crossed the narrow hallway to my neighbour's door, which was ajar. I kicked it wider, ready for conflict. The bed was made, the curtains open. I pulled out

head back on the lounger again and closed my eyes. Logic and reason. Brim and a Maigret novel. What did they have in common? I checked the spine of the book. There was nothing that could have been concealed by Churchill's toy shop at The Firs. There just wasn't room. My mind drifted ...

"Have you been asleep, Jovencita? Come on, we dock in an hour. Let's have a drink." I had been dreaming about Maria and the children as well. Her favourite red wine smelt rank in the shadows that danced in my mind. An ominous portent? And Sophie Vidal had played a central role in my tangled web of dreams too: a girl of around my age, cut down in the prime of her life by a savage who might well be a lot more than just Henri, my neighbour. I felt an enormous amount of empathy towards Sophie, a girl I never knew, who had just been in the wrong place at the wrong time.

the dazzling sun. Tiny specks floated in the aqueous fluid of my eyes as my mind wandered back to meeting Freddie Valentine for the first time at the Queen Victoria Hospital. So long ago now, it seemed. My mind drifted; it was the motion of the boat. Thinking of Freddie reminded me suddenly of Beaulieu, the Alvis and the drive in the New Forest.

I took the book Freddie had given me, from Brim, out of my bag and admired the cover: La Maison du Juge. I still hadn't had the time to read it. I flicked through the pages of the Georges Simenon novel from back to front and found a solitary inscription: P.A.D. I repeated the exercise, wondering what it meant and why he had he given it to me. Was there something significant within the text?

The novel was printed in French and had been published in France, 1940. A pristine first edition. I flicked through the pages once more, with growing confusion. It had come from Brim, that much Freddie had told me, so somewhere within these pages was a message. A clue. But where? I flicked through the pages once more, carefully scanning. And then a thought occurred to me: I drew the book near to my face – Brim's old ruse – and sniffed the pages. Ah, I smiled. There were deposits of cigar ash trapped against the seam of two pages. Up close the smell was quite pungent. I noted their numbers.

67, 91

a political poster or in a newspaper before the war when I was on a walking holiday, south of Munich on the Austrian border. But I can't remember his name. It's not Himmler or Göring. But he was certainly high-ranking SS, or perhaps even Gestapo."

This raised the possibility that my neighbour was not only the killer of Sophie Vidal – I was certain of that – but also a war criminal. I had only seen file photos of some of the Wehrmacht, Luftwaffe and Kriegsmarine. Many of the faces were of public figures – Dönitz, Rommel and Goebbels. This man's name and identity were unknown to me.

"Oh yes, Jovencita. If I am correct, this man has ordered the extermination of thousands of innocent people. Families torn apart by some Ayran philosophy. Some crazy, nightmare vision." Orfila had been solemn and dismal as we had left the railway station and headed towards the boat to take us home.

*

Our return journey to Villaricos was a lot less exciting than the voyage out. The excitement that comes from being on a mission was distinctly absent. Finding the newspaper hadn't helped Orfila's mood at all. Or mine for that matter; I was deflated. Orfila was preoccupied and kept himself to himself, locked away in his cabin for most of the voyage south. We only met at mealtimes or on deck. A solitary question hung in the air unanswered: what should we do when we returned to Villaricos?

Voyage

The Mediterranean.

MY MIND DRIFTED AS I SAT back on the deck of the boat on our voyage back. A number of questions crossed my mind:

What had Orfila meant by: My God, I have seen that face before. I had absolutely no idea. He had been sitting on the wooden bench beside me in the waiting room at the railway station in Barcelona, still clutching Le Figaro and staring at the photograph of the scene at the hotel in Arles.

He had been transfixed. “You realise, I have never actually seen this Henri character in Villaricos,” Orfila had said quietly, “but I am sure the man in this photograph is a former Nazi. If he was in France – as he is in this image – and now he is in Spain – he must be on the run. Escaped from Germany.”

“What?” The initial shock began to wane as his words sank in. A former Nazi? Escaped? So, my earlier assumptions may have been right. Military, Nazi or political? I feared that my money was on a senior political figure. But how senior?

underwater for more than two minutes; you name it; can't abide moths. Strange."

Villiers turned and left the office without another word, leaving Penfold slightly bemused by the whole thing. He wanted to ask a question but decided not to.

"Ilex Aquifolium," muttered Brim, "holly hedge. I knew it would come to me."

Penfold packed his pipe paraphernalia back into its little chamois pouch. "Was it true about the moths, Brim?"

"Oh yes," said Brim, deadpan. "She was attacked by a swarm of them as a toddler. Never been the same since, according to her parents."

Once again, Penfold couldn't tell if he was joking or not. Someone had once perceptively said that Brim was impossible to read: the ultimate bluffer, the gambler who never gambled. What had he just got himself into?

"Hmm," Villiers continued, "I'll check with Records, local geography and logistics. We will need to obtain transport somehow once we get there. Shouldn't be too difficult, with a bundle of pesetas! ..." He paused again ... "Oh and I'll need two men from RAF Special Investigations Branch. Is that all right?"

This was what Brim had wanted and intended all along:

"Yes. I'll get onto Squadron Leader Squires at Northolt, Freddie Valentine's old CO. Perfect man for the job. He can arrange high security clearance for the flight crew and charter. I'll sanction fuel and overtime from Central Funding. Nobody else must know of this mission," said Brim bluntly. "We want Müller terminated. No fuss. No tribunals. Need to know."

He opened his desk drawer and pulled out a 10"x8" black and white file photo of Lucy: a copy of the one in her French CNI document. He handed it to Villiers. "Do you need this?" asked Brim. He already knew the answer.

Villiers took the photograph and studied it for thirty seconds or so. "No, it's fine. That's a face I won't forget in a hurry." He handed it back to Brim, who placed it back in the drawer.

Brim smiled and stood up from his chair and walked around his desk: "Then I won't detain you."

Brim shook Villiers' hand. Villiers stood back and saluted. He looked like a man ready to run a marathon, champing at the bit.

"By the way. What is the thing Lucy fears most?" Villiers asked Brim.

"Moths," said Brim with a chuckle. "She has an irrational

monster like that. The more we learn about these Nazi death camps, the more disgusted we are. Talk about man's inhumanity to man. And there'll be more revelations to come, mark my words." The flow of conversation ceased for a moment.

Villiers stood. "I think what Brim is saying is that we don't need to involve the Americans or the Russians. The less General Pritchard knows, the better. And as for General Zhukov, he'd send the entire Red Army down there if he got wind of this. No, this is the right decision – kill the enemy and liberate Lucy from Spain." He paused and looked at Penfold.

"I read the summary you gave me of her time in SOE, Brim. Lucy's role in Bordeaux was a triumph of espionage and courage. We need to pull her out. She's done enough. She must be physically and mentally exhausted, poor girl. It's time."

"We're agreed then?" Brim looked at the two men. This was a unique and delicate situation; and they all knew it.

"It looks like it," said Penfold without conviction, poking the embers in the bowl of his pipe absent-mindedly.

"Colonel Penfold," said Brim formally, "I need your commitment and your full support on this one."

There was another extended silence. "You have it, of course," said Penfold finally. There was a tone of reluctance in his voice.

Villiers' face cracked into a smile. "We'll need to requisition a Lysander to fly us from Northolt to Spain. I happen to know there's a naval seaplane training base at Murcia. Not far from Villaricos, from there on by road."

The question had provoked an air of awkwardness, which Villiers dispelled with his courtroom manner. “What do you wish to do, Professor?” he asked carefully. “How do you wish this matter to be, well, handled?” Despite the slowness of his question, he wanted answers.

“How would you feel about taking a flight to Spain, Villiers?” asked Brim casually, as if he didn’t care how Villiers felt.

Villiers licked his lips, sensing opportunities. “To see Hobson, do you mean?”

Brim glanced briefly at Penfold. This was crucial. “No,” said Brim finally, “to go to Villaricos and find Lucy. That shouldn’t be hard for a man of your talents. Oh, and get shot of Heinrich Müller while you’re at it.”

Villiers’ eyes lit up, the sinews of his neck taut. Müller had murdered more than a hundred of his colleagues at Stalag Luft; he was a war criminal who thought he was on course to escape justice. This was a chance for revenge, and Villiers could almost taste it.

Penfold simulated an expression of shock, as if he had never contemplated such a notion. “Are you asking me to sanction an unauthorised kill?”

“Yes,” said Brim with conviction. He suddenly altered the tenor of his voice. “That is to say, you are party to a group decision to issue a kill order.”

“Group decision?” Penfold chewed his lip, feigning concern.

“Or Villiers could simply pop down to Spain, arrest him and

rule: the fewer who know, the better. Hobson betrayed that request, by following up with that telegram. But at least he chose his words carefully." Brim peered out of the window. He could picture a sumptuous office in the Embassy; Henry pouring on the charm, Lucy being evasive. That was her. At least, that was her training.

"Does it matter?" asked Villiers, glancing at his watch, breaking into Brim's daydream.

"Yes. It means he senses she is in danger. I am tempted to telephone him, but I won't risk it. The Consulate over there could compromised. Switchboard staff, however carefully vetted, can never be fully trusted. They are open to bribery, temptation. You know the situation, I'm sure. All the staff are ex-army, trained at Sandhurst." Brim went on to say that Hobson, as a diplomat in a foreign country, was probably not quite sure who to trust. His caution was wise, he was trying to protect Lucy. She must have confided in him to some extent in order to gain his trust and co-operation. The two visitors listened, but Villiers was clearly keen to move on. Brim might give the impression that he was stalling, but that was far from the truth: it was the way he played the game.

"Would Hobson have opened the cylinder, Brim?" asked Penfold. He immediately knew he shouldn't have asked such an indiscreet question.

Brim frowned, his face dark: "I would say not, John. Trust is paramount. That's not to say he wasn't curious; he certainly

you know Consul-General Hobson, Brim?" He took out his briar and began the lengthy process of filling and lighting it. Strands of loose tobacco fell out of a curious-looking chamois pouch which was perched on his lap, but he did not seem to notice.

Brim turned from the window and sighed: "He was just Henry Hobson when I met him at the Embassy in Paris at a day's pow-wow in '38, so not very well at all really. But I seem to recall he had an extraordinarily beautiful wife. She was Spanish, if memory serves, with the most unbelievably green eyes. Decent enough fellow though, I should imagine. You must be, to advance in those diplomatic circles. He was a Cambridge man, as I recall, King's."

Villiers picked up the telegram and read it aloud: "'Trust the package arrived safely. The sender was emphatic that it must be sent to you direct. Regards, Henry.' Thoughts, Brim?" He might have been cross-examining a witness in court.

Brim emitted a customary chuckle. "It's what it doesn't say, old sport: it's neutral. The choice of words, you see. 'The package' – not 'cylinder', and 'the sender' – not 'she'. It's as if Henry assumed something might get back to the wrong person; a person who might be a danger to her."

"And?" asked Villiers. He shifted in his seat as if he wanted to move on.

"It bears all the hallmarks of Lucy: caution and discretion," said Brim after a moment. "She would have told Hobson firmly: no communication with London – just send it to Professor

Villiers

British Intelligence, London, England.

A FEW DAYS LATER Brim stood at the window of his office in London and studied the holly hedge in the small, enclosed garden. His inability to recall its Latin name irritated him, but he did have plenty on his mind. On his desk lay the telegram Miss Trueblood, his devoted secretary, had delivered only a few hours earlier. Seated in leather armchairs were Colonel John Penfold, the British Army Berlin Resident and Miles Villiers of RAF Special Investigations Branch, whose muscular build seemed to challenge every seam of his pre-war suit.

Villiers' impenetrable eyes and inscrutable countenance gave little away. His receding hairline and Roman nose gave his face a distinctive, almost aristocratic look. Many of the female staff at RAF/SIB at Cranwell had a thing for Villiers, particularly an RT operator called Rosie Walker, but he either didn't notice or pretended not to. Even with Villiers' imperious, slightly arrogant manner, Brim knew he could trust him. He'd have to.

danger. Grave danger."

"We could send an RAF Special Investigation Branch aircraft down there. Miles Villiers would be more than happy to provide an intercept team," Penfold suggested.

Brim waited for some time before he responded. "Müller would recognise the sound of an enemy aircraft a mile off and run. Then we'd definitely never find him." He sighed: "But we could send Villiers without his full team. He's tough and resourceful."

"Under the radar, so to speak?" suggested Penfold.

Brim smiled and turned off the lamp. "Exactly, John. Spot on."

information are extraordinary. She's given us a face, possible intelligence and a place. The dispatch from Hobson was dated three days ago." Brim went on to explain that Lucy must have an instinct that the man was of significance. "He's German and he's in Spain. Who knows? Even now, few people recognise the faces and appearance of senior Gestapo and SS members, particularly people outside Germany. The question is, what do we do next?"

"Do you think she's in danger?" asked Penfold. In a way, it was a stupid question, because it was all about context. And Brim knew this and knew Penfold was still shocked by what he had seen.

"Only if he finds out who Lucy really is. It depends on the nature of their encounter. And, crucially, the length of it. If Müller was in Villaricos, he could be in transit to somewhere else."

"Yes, most likely," Penfold sniffed nervously.

Brim huffed, leant back and clasped his hands behind his neck. A minute or so passed before he spoke again. "The report from your meeting with Villiers, Zhukov and Pritchard indicated that you believed Müller was heading west – your words, I think, John – to Spain and then North Africa."

"Yes." Penfold took out his customary briar and started filling it with tobacco. "Then the encounter could have been brief or lengthy; we've no way of knowing."

"Lucy would just need enough time to absorb Müller's features and memorise them. Committing them to paper would

Gibraltar, or the Embassy. Her Spanish is competent and, most importantly, she understands the system."

"She sounds extraordinary," said Penfold respectfully. "And there is no question that it was she who sketched this image?"

"None whatsoever," said Brim. "The combination of caution and the ingenuity are quite characteristic."

Penfold nodded, impressed at what he had heard so far about Lucy Fry. He glanced at Brim, who was studying her communiqué in detail.

"For example, have a look at the shadowing on the right-hand side of the image. You'll need this." Brim handed Penfold a powerful magnifying glass.

Penfold unfurled the sheet and flattened it on the desk, weighing the corners down with scissors, inkpot and whatever else came to hand. He inspected the shading carefully and said nothing for a few minutes. Outside the rain was pouring down and the room went dark. Brim flicked on an Anglepoise lamp, creating a pool of light over the desk. Penfold read the tiny words, "Villaricos. Spain. I believe this man is German. Overheard telephone call: 'I need money for engine parts and fuel.'"

"Is there any way Lucy could know exactly who she is dealing with here?"

Brim pursed his lips. "No. I don't believe so, hence her caution. And she doesn't want to lose sight of him for longer than she must."

it were somehow contaminated. Ridiculous, really, he would think later.

Brim swivelled round in his chair and looked out of the window. He spoke reflectively in a low voice, almost as if he were talking to himself and reaffirming all the facts.

"We have an agent, nicknamed The Artist; excellent linguist and photographer; and as you can see, a skilled artist. Her name is Lucy Fry."

"The agent is a woman?" asked Penfold. Most of the agents he'd heard about – or met – were men.

Brim turned the chair back to face Penfold: "Yes. Back in February '44 she was assigned an undercover mission to Bordeaux. I won't trouble you with the details, but it was a pretty grim task. The mission was a success, but suffice it to say, she had to get out, PDQ. For a while we thought she was dead, fleeing the Gestapo."

"But she wasn't?"

Brim sighed: "No. We finally received a signal from her via a Wireless Operator in the Tarbes network: WHEELWRIGHT. It was one of Leo's poem codes, so we knew it was genuine." Brim went on to explain that he knew Lucy had reached Spain. The signal to Major Pelham at Poundon – though brief – had been to let Brim know she was alive and that her mission had been accomplished. She had since been instructed by him – and SOE Norgeby House – to remain in Spain.

"Why?" asked Penfold.

Penfold picked it up, pulled out a large sheet of sketch paper and carefully unrolled it. The pencilled image on the paper clearly shocked him. "Where on earth did you get this?" he asked quietly.

"The British Consulate in Barcelona via the Consul-General, Sir Henry A. Hobson. Diplomatic bag, a few days ago. Hence the rush."

"I can't believe it. It's – it's the face of Heinrich Müller, Gestapo." Brim nodded as Penfold continued. "The only person to have escaped the Führerbunker – at least, the only one not yet accounted for."

"There is no question, is there?" asked Brim solemnly. "I mean that it's him."

"No. This is an accurate sketch, there is no doubt at all, Brim."

Brim pressed on, "You saw the man at close quarters at the '36 Olympics, and a few other times before the war?"

Penfold composed himself: "There's no question; it's him." Brim heard the tremor in his voice.

They both knew the significance of this development. Müller was a sadistic monster who had pitilessly caused untold misery and suffering to so many people. He was as bad as Himmler if that was possible. And here was his face, clear as day.

"I'm sorry to press you, John. I had to make absolutely sure I wasn't imagining things," said Brim in a perceptive tone.

"I understand, of course. It was just a bit of a shock," said

extensive knowledge of political history, literature and poetry. He appreciated the work of Shakespeare and Conan Doyle and had read all the Georges Simenon novels in their original French.

Churchill's secret military defence laboratory (MD1), was in the village of Whitchurch in Buckinghamshire, a little to the north of the capital. MD1 had covertly requisitioned The Firs, a country mansion, which was ideal for its purposes. Brimblecombe was sitting behind his desk looking at an eighteen-inch cardboard cylinder with various stamps and seals adorning its surface. There was a knock on the door, and Brimblecombe shouted, "Come."

Colonel Penfold stepped into the room wearing full military uniform with his cap tucked under his arm and a beige mackintosh draped over his shoulders. He was utterly soaked, but the resemblance to Montgomery persisted. "Damned filthy out there today, Brim." He took off the wet mackintosh and hung it on a bentwood hat stand with his army cap. Rivulets of rainwater dripped into a metal collection tray at the base.

Brimblecombe – Brim – as he was known to the privileged few stood and shook Penfold's hand.

"Good to see you, John. Sorry about the rush, but I knew you'd want to see this, pronto." Brim's summons had brought Penfold at short notice from Berlin to RAF Northolt, then he had been driven up to Whitchurch by Military Police Transport. Without further ado, Brim pointed at the cardboard cylinder.

Brim

Churchill's Toy Shop, Whitchurch, Buckinghamshire, England.

PROFESSOR NICHOLAS BRIMBLECOMBE, eminent academic and connoisseur of the finer things of life, was very well connected. As head of British Intelligence, he was the ultimate spymaster. In his capacity as European Chief of Operations he had a network of contacts from Basle to Washington DC, and the sanction of the PM to authorise certain coercive measures when 'deemed necessary'. This had been acutely so during wartime.

Brimblecombe was an amalgam of different personas, with a combination of skills to suit whatever situation – or crisis – he found himself in. He made robust decisions, and he supported the people he trusted without fail. And they, in turn, trusted him. His vices were few: he enjoyed a single malt and appreciated a fine claret, but he was by no means a serious drinker. He was selective and careful. He smoked, but not to excess. His personal life, for security reasons, was shrouded in mystery. A double first

was Sophie's killer.

Suddenly everything was clear. That was why he was uncommunicative. He was a man with more than one secret. Did José and Maria know they were harbouring a killer? Should I go to the police? Should I go back to the Consulate? What would they do? What evidence did I have? What real options? No. I should return to Villaricos, confront Henri with the article and see how he reacted. I wasn't scared of him: I had eaten tougher men than him for breakfast.

Orfila returned from the ticket office with two return rail tickets to Girona. He handed one to me and his face crinkled into his familiar smile. "There we are Lucy. A present from Orfila. A return ticket to Girona."

"I'm sorry," I said sadly, "The visit's off. I just can't go." He looked upset so I handed him the crumpled copy of Le Figaro. "Look at the picture. The man on the far side. Do you recognize him?"

He sat down on the wooden bench beside me; his face a dark shadow: "My God, I have seen that face before."

I assumed he had recognised the man as my neighbour, Henri. He hadn't. For him, it was somebody else completely. I had absolutely no idea then of the terrible shock that awaited me.

Orfila had assured me was enchanting, was a hundred miles to the north. The idea sounded good and so I agreed. That I would probably never go there again was my rationale.

Left on a bench in the waiting room, presumably by a passenger who had travelled to Barcelona from France, was an old copy of Le Figaro. It was a little creased, but perfectly readable. I saw the article and its accompanying photograph by sheer chance. The headline was:

WAITRESS SLAIN IN ARLES.

And the article explained that Sophie Vidal, a waitress at Hôtel La Maison Jaune in the town centre, had been brutally murdered by an unknown person.

The photograph was of the courtyard and an open-fronted bar at the hotel in Arles. Two celebrities from Paris, Jean-Pierre Raimbault and Didier Pourcel, were visiting Arles - where Van Gogh had briefly lived - as part of a publicity tour. It was all to promote Pourcel's newly published book: VINCENT – A Portrait.

They were seated in the foreground looking suitably avant-garde, signing books and enjoying the limelight. To one side of the celebrated pair was Sophie Vidal, the victim, the article explained. She was striking in a Garboesque way, in a white blouse and black pinafore; a sexy-looking girl in her mid-twenties. The same age as me. On the other side of the picture, caught by a wide-angle lens, was an unnamed man who may have believed that he was out of shot. I knew the eyes, the

Le Figaro

Café Biarritz, Barcelona, Spain.

ORFILA WAS SITTING AT A TABLE OUTSIDE a small café on a side street near the British Consulate. I walked twice around the block before joining him. There was no sign of a tail, but you can never be entirely certain. I was tired, and when tired I was prone to clumsiness. I smiled nervously.

"What would you like?" Orfila asked me courteously. He offered me a chair in the shade of an umbrella. "The coffee is rich and strong, unlike me." He chuckled at his little joke and watched me carefully, like a doctor studying a patient.

"Nothing," I said quickly. "Let's go." He could obviously see that I was anxious. The meeting, though positive, had sapped me. In fact, I was just desperate to get away from the environs of the Consulate. He finished his coffee in a single gulp and stood, leaving some coins on the table. I thanked him as he took my arm, and we were away.

As a treat, Orfila had persuaded me that we should take the

took the cylinder, perhaps surprised by its lightness, and smiled warmly, weighing it in his hands. I could see he was wondering what could be inside it.

"Thank you," I said, relieved to be finally rid of it and confident that Sir Henry would do as he had promised.

"In fact, you are a very courageous young lady. I admire your fortitude; SOE, MI6... extraordinary work you all did during the war. And, clearly after it." This time I merely nodded my thanks."You've done well. How long have you been in Spain?" He rotated the cardboard cylinder in his hands.

I sighed and thought back. "I fled Tarbes in February '44. So, a long time. I found an apartment in Villaricos and have been there ever since. I am helping a young family – José and Maria Cordera, and Maria's two children, Antonio and Ana. They pay for my keep and a little extra."

Hobson smiled: "You can't stay there forever, can you? What will you do?"

"I hope that cylinder you are holding will give me the answer to that question. I want to go home, Sir Henry. I've had enough."

It was the first time I had admitted it, even to myself. There was nothing more to be said. He held out his hand and I shook it firmly, the way my father had always taught me to do. I let myself out of the Consul-General's office and was escorted off the premises by the same armed guard who had admitted me – I glanced at my watch – I had been with Hobson for just under an hour. There was no sign of the unfortunate Mr. Avery.

"I had help from the Resistance in Tarbes to escape to Spain. I trusted them." I cleared my throat; my mouth was dry with nerves. This was the first time I had explained the peculiar position I found myself in. In a way it was quite cathartic. "Can you help me, please?"

I could hear Hobson swallow and see the rise and fall of his Adam's apple. I had shocked him by trampling my muddy shoes on his pristine white carpet. Suddenly I felt tired, as if my confession had drained me of substance.

"Of course, I will help you, Miss Fry." Hobson sounded a little breathless.

"Lucy," I said softly. I had changed from an innocent French citizen in need of emergency assistance into what I was: a survivor; a spy and a killer who had been trained by the best. "I want this cylinder sent to Professor Brimblecombe, and I would like your personal assurance it will be sent soonest. You are my one hope." Hobson handed me back my CNI card and I handed him the cylinder. This was more than just an exchange of physical items; it cemented an understanding. "Your personal assurance, Sir Henry," I said again before I released the cylinder from my grasp, and I emphasised the word personal.

"You have it."

"No contact with London. No telephone calls or telegrams. Don't mention my name to anyone. Or this conversation. Just send the messenger. The shorter the chain, the better. Isn't that the golden rule of espionage?"

I took another deep breath. “My target was Commander Dieter Heller, U-Boat Commander North Atlantic, based in Bordeaux. He was responsible for sinking more shipping than any other commander. My instructions were clear – find him – and, well I am sure you can guess the rest. Expedient demise. Teach the bloody Germans a lesson. Crack their morale.”

“And did you?”

“Yes. In a rented house in Bordeaux – near the U-Boat pens – it wasn’t easy. I had to gain his trust first, over the course of many weeks and then ... well, you can imagine – a seduction that wasn’t too obviously contrived and planned by British Intelligence. The only saving grace in the whole appalling story is that I know Heller had planned to kill me the night I escaped from Bordeaux.”

“Gosh.”

“He had a stiletto strapped to his leg. But I got him first.”

Hobson looked even more shocked. “It must have affected you, having to kill someone like that. Someone you had...” He stumbled.

“Slept with? Is that what you mean?” I couldn’t help but raise my voice. “Yes. It did affect me. But I pictured in my mind the image of wolfpacks of U-Boats ambushing British and American ships and thousands of servicemen and civilians dead in the Atlantic. That’s what I focused on... so, yes, that’s...” I took a deep breath, “That’s all I had.”

“I’m sorry,” Hobson said contritely.

What was in the cylinder? And what was a twenty-seven-year-old woman doing in this predicament?

He arched an eyebrow and planted two thumbs into his waistcoat pockets. "Miss Fry, I am a little confused. The war is over." He paused. "Can't you just take it there yourself? There are a few flights to London now via Paris. Or do you need money? I can make you a small advance, at least HM Government can, if you are in a pickle."

"No. For compelling reasons I can't afford to be absent from where I'm staying for too long. And I have orders to remain in Spain until instructed otherwise. But thank you, it is most kind."

"Not at all. You obviously have your reasons." He offered me a seat, which I declined. I had to be firm but respectful. And stay on his level. "I sense you have been through a lot, Miss Fry. Would it help to talk about it?" He smiled for the first time and I could see why he was a diplomat: he was simultaneously gracious and wary. I had to be careful, but I had to be honest.

I took a breath: "Among other things, back in February 1944, I killed two SS patrollers while on the run from Bordeaux in a stolen Reich-owned car. I set up a fake roadblock and shot them. I ran, and I've kept on running, Sir Henry. What I need now is your help."

Hobson looked shocked; I wondered for a moment whether he had a daughter of about my age. I went on to explain about my role in Bordeaux gathering intelligence about the long-range submarines of the Kriegsmarine and the Italian navy patrolling

announced in a crisp BBC accent as if reading the shipping forecast, "and I am English."

Hobson looked more surprised than shocked. "I see."

"I work for Professor Nicholas Brimblecombe, British Intelligence. I can see from your expression that his name rings a bell. Is that correct, Sir Henry?"

Hobson pursed his lips in a manner reminiscent of Brimblecombe. Whether this was intentional or not was hard to say: "I know who he is, of course. What do you wish to see me about, Miss Fry?"

I suddenly thought of the man I had seen outside and lowered my voice. "I'll come to that if I may. But tell me, who is the man in the morning suit?"

"Oh, that's Simon, Simon Avery. The poor chap had a terrible accident during army manoeuvres; lost a leg and sustained shrapnel wounds to his jaw and shoulder, on Salisbury Plain of all places. One or two – ah – shall we say mental issues too. Like shell shock."

"Blown up by his own side?" I asked with a trace of irony. Poor bugger.

"Quite," he said with a trace of exasperation that I hadn't anticipated.

I realised I had to up my game. I reckoned I had ten more seconds to convince him before he called the gatehouse guard. "Do you have a diplomatic bag that cannot be opened by Spanish officials – a King's Messenger - to take this cylinder to London?"

years as a nurse, and the instruments he was carrying didn't ring alarm bells, as he gave the impression of someone behaving quite normally. I didn't look closely enough to notice the expression in his eyes.

*

As soon as I entered Hobson's shuttered colonial-style office, I could see him eyeing me up and down as if admiring a new car. I read his look: a combination of lust, interest and puzzlement. He was a wiry stick-insect of a fellow who seemed totally ill-placed in the almost tropical Spanish heat. He sported a black toothbrush moustache reminiscent of Neville Chamberlain's and spoke like an ageing headmaster. His three-piece suit and Cambridge University tie only reinforced the air of academia, but there was charm in his manner.

"So, what can I do, Mademoiselle Claude Moreau?" he asked stiffly, clearly not entirely comfortable about being alone with a woman half his age. "This is a British Consulate, not French. But given our special post-war relationship ..." He let his words trail off. He was holding my CNI card and spoke perfect French. "23b rue Ramey, Clignancourt. I used to work in Paris, at the Embassy. Happiest times of my life, I think. Ah, Montmartre! The Left Bank!" He daydreamed for a moment: "Well now, the gatehouse guard said it was an emergency. Pray, do tell."

Stupidly, I hadn't prepared for this conversation, just how to

Hobson

British Consulate, Barcelona, Spain.

WE MADE IT TO THE British Consulate in Barcelona in slightly under two days. The Consul-General, Sir Henry A. Hobson, agreed to see me without question. To the gatehouse guard I must have appeared desperate, anxious, convincing and, if I am honest, a little flirtatious, because I knew that would work. I was passed from the guard to a tall, dark and surly man inside the Consulate who said simply, "Please to – follow me." We walked down a corridor into a circular reception area, ahead of which was a pair of tall, ornate-looking doors.

Out of the corner of my eye I just about registered the presence of a hollow-faced man whose appearance seemed a little incongruous in these surroundings. His face was badly disfigured, and he was wearing a morning suit despite the heat. He was standing outside another pair of tall doors holding a length of coiled telephone cable, several screwdrivers and a pair of pliers. Why would a man in such formal dress be carrying an

and yours ... distant cousins?" I laughed. Dammit, I was a little tipsy. "Lucy? I like that name," he continued. "It suits you better than Claude."

I stood and helped clear the last few things away: the jars of pickles, the olive oil and the bread board, and corked the bottle of dangerous wine. "Why are you going to help me, Orfila?"

Orfila turned from his kitchen chores and looked at me. He seemed to be composing his words – justifying his decision in his own mind. "I am Spanish. Of course I support Franco, El Caudillo! This is for Spain. Still, I hated Hitler and the Nazi regime. The Third Reich was evil and deserved to be defeated."

I tried to act naturally, "So?"

He waited and then said, "The purpose of your visit to Barcelona concerns your neighbour – the German – yes?" I nodded, shocked. Orfila smiled and continued, "Yes. My sister works at the Post Office. She has overheard several telephone calls. The same as you did."

"I see."

"And you make regular calls to France. The connection is to Tarbes, yes?"

There was little point in denying it. "Yes. I do."

"And I'll tell you something else, Lucy." This time I waited. "Henri – or whatever his name is – paid José Cordera a lot of money to hide him."

"I see. Does Maria know?"

"How could she not?" Orfila said finally.

triumph on his lined old face.

"Yes," I conceded and laughed at the way he had emphasised 'we'.

He sat back, like a man who had just won a hand at cards, "I am a man of the world, Jovencita. I do not wish to know all your personal business but, somehow you got into Spain. And not with a British passport, no? Some other papers – originally at one of the French borders, eh?"

"Yes, with French papers. As you know, my name is Claude Moreau," I said emphatically.

"And yet you are English?" He narrowed his shrewd old eyes, like an inquisitor.

"Who says?" I felt a little drunk and irritated at how easily he had caught me out. The subject of my nationality had not been raised until now. I poured more water.

"Come now, we have known each other too long for untruths." Touché.

There was nothing I could do, and he had to know the real story. "Alright then. My real name is Lucy Fry," I said embarrassed. "I am a doctor's daughter from Devon, in England. Bovey Tracey to be precise."

"Maybe you are," Orfila said with a doubtful smile.

He could have added that this still didn't explain who I really was and what I was doing in Villaricos, but he didn't. He stood and cleared the dishes, saying matter-of-factly, "We will drive to Cartagena on Tuesday and stay at an inn near Mazarrón on the

Barcelona is by sea. Unless you have horses, paid helpers and carriages, and are unrestricted by time like the Crusaders."

"By sea?" I mulled the idea over. Of course, by sea. That made perfect sense; the ferry I had travelled on myself a year ago.

Orfila stood and went to a large sink, turned on a single tap and washed his hands, drying them meticulously with a fresh towel. "Relations between Spain and Britain are not so good, because of the war; you know this, I am sure."

I watched him as he carefully folded the towel. He went on to say that a UN resolution had excluded Spain from membership of many international organisations, leaving it isolated. The Spanish police and security forces would be suspicious of an attractive (his word) woman travelling alone, and I knew this from my escape from France.

"Suspicious?" I repeated.

He looked doleful as he returned to his chair; the wooden legs scraped on the slab stone floor. "Si. Suspicious. Unusual. There have been no tourists since the war ended. Spanish women of your age would not travel without a husband or other male relative. Certainly not alone." I drank more wine and he decanted some water into my glass as he had done with his own. The dilution was a blessing as my head was starting to swim, just a little. "What papers are you travelling with?" His crafty old eyes twinkled as he confidently wheedled information out of me.

"We would not be leaving Spain, surely?" I questioned, my

I sighed, calculating the distance and thought to myself: Three hundred and ninety miles? That's a hell of a long way. He beckoned me to sit, poured a spot more wine and broke bread, ever the priest.

"Could I get there by road? Train?" I suggested. God, but it was strong wine!

"Why do you wish to go?" Orfila asked again. He frowned, and his chestnut-coloured face cracked into a thousand wrinkles, like an old leather glove. Then his frown melted into a smile, his blue eyes sparkled in the low light.

This was not a man to be lied to. I had to trust him. But what could he possibly do to help me? I came straight out with it, "I have to get a package to the Consul-General at the British Consulate in Barcelona."

Orfila sniffed, drank some wine, cut some cold ham and placed several slices on my plate with olives, pickles and fresh peppers, and gestured for me to help myself. He waited, his cautious old eyes level as he looked at me. "You are not a simple housemaid and teacher to the Cordera family, are you, Jovencita?"

"No."

"You are hiding, maybe waiting, yes?" He chuckled, sighed, "But waiting for whom, or for what, eh?" I remained silent as we started to eat our lunch. Orfila drank some of his wine and poured water from a decanter into his glass, diluting its contents to the colour of some tropical fruit juice. "No matter. You can tell

Young lady would do, I thought, although that wasn't entirely accurate either.

"How far is Barcelona from here?" I asked suddenly, dreading the answer.

Orfila whistled, looked at his watch and smiled, "It is lunchtime." He turned from the pharmacy counter, walked to the door and pulled the blind down. The shop fell into darkness and he clicked the lock, "Follow me." We walked from the back of the shop down a few stone steps into his modest kitchen. Without a word he started to prepare cold meat, tomatoes, salad, olives, pickles and bread, and poured two glasses of Rioja. In the centre of the room there was a heavy wooden table bearing the marks of a hundred years of culinary use. Orfila produced a map of Spain from shelves stacked with recipes and pharmaceutical journals. He eyed me quizzically, "Why do you wish to go?"

"Personal business," I said quickly. "I have to deliver a present." It sounded blunt and felt rude; he didn't deserve to be treated like a fool. I bit my tongue, regretting it.

The look in Orfila's eyes said he didn't believe me. But, like the priest he resembled, he chose to say nothing. He unfolded the map on the table, exposing the south-east region of the country. It was a huge area. I had almost forgotten just how vast a country Spain was. My escape from France was a long time ago.

"Cartagena – Torrevieja – Valencia – Castellón de la Plana – Tarragona – Barcelona." He ran a blunt forefinger along the

Orfila

Pharmacy. Villaricos, Spain.

DR.ORFILA HAD BECOME an unexpected ally. More than that, he was a confidant and a friend. On first meeting I had thought him solemn, but he was quite the reverse. His bedside manner was formal and professional, but with me he was lively and engaging. When we were alone, we communicated in Spanish, French and English. The conversations helped us both. I had made many return visits to Orfila, as he now wished me to call him. Initially they had been for additional medical supplies for Ana so I could tend her wounded knee, and then I ran out of excuses. I went there for coffee and companionship. There was really no-one else who met that need in me, and I liked him immensely. My creation had been inspired, but the problem still lay in getting it safely back to London.

"Something is wrong, Jovencita?" Orfila asked when I paid him a late morning visit. We were standing in the cool of the pharmacy; he seemed to read my mood. Jovencita, he had

suspicious – he knew I had a camera, and he would probably guess my motive. My only real option was to set up a candid shot. I would have to get up before he did and hide so I could catch him when he left with his fishing gear, but there would probably be insufficient light at that hour to give a sharp enough image. I worked through the logistics as I walked back to the villa, breathless from the heat. I thought of the children and our games with drawings and laughed out loud. How stupid! I looked down at my hands; the answer was right in front of me. I could surely create something. My mind was a whirl of ideas. The problem would be getting that something back to Brim in London.

"Thank you, I am French. I also speak English, but I am still learning Spanish." I may have blushed.

"Would you prefer to speak French, or English."

"I would prefer to practice my Spanish," I said in French, and he laughed. My little witticism seemed to amuse him. "All right, but where was I? Oh yes, I think I said I assumed, didn't I?"

"Ah yes. But it is a dangerous thing to do, to assume," he continued. He stopped and looked over his pince-nez as if deciding whether to reveal more. "José and Antonio were great friends. They had a terrible flying accident. You must have noticed the scars on José's face." He pointed at his own forehead and temples. "At least he lived. Antonio did not. His body had 90% burns – the hospital could not save him. They did not have the necessary knowledge and, yes, special dressings."

He pushed the items across the counter to me and smiled dolefully, "No charge."

I nodded, thanked him and walked out of the pharmacy into the sunlight. That explained so much about the domestic arrangements of the villa. So, Maria was a widow. But why all the secrecy? In all the months I had spent in her house, she had never mentioned a husband. I made my way back to the villa, clutching the bandages, and iodine for Ana.

Then I stopped in my tracks. You are the guest staying with Maria Cordera. A statement, not a question; singular, not plural. So why didn't he say – one of the guests? There were two of us. It didn't make sense. Why didn't he mention Henri? I needed a

*

This was my first visit to the pharmacy in Villaricos, which was just off the main square. Dr. Mathieu Orfila, the prescribing pharmacist, sported pince-nez and a grey goatee beard. He listened to my account of the problem like a priest hearing confession. Framed certificates on the wall proclaimed his qualifications from the University of Barcelona, and Dr. Orfila proved to be an educated and articulate man.

"You are the guest staying with Maria Cordera," he said with accuracy, "so the 'little girl' you speak of must be Ana." It wasn't a question; he obviously knew the family. Villaricos was a small town. He turned to select what he needed from the shelves behind him.

"Yes. They are a very pleasant couple. And lovely children," I said innocently.

He placed some plain gauze bandages and a bottle of iodine solution onto the long wooden counter.

"Couple, no. They are brother and sister. Maria's husband, the father of the children, died two years ago. Antonio López was very popular. I knew him well."

Then I thought of the name of the villa: Residencia López-Cordera. I must have looked astonished; I certainly felt it.

"Cordera is the family name." He frowned, his face sad.

"I – I assumed..."

"You are obviously not Spanish," he said graciously, "but

*

A sudden loud knock on the front door of the villa interrupted our secret pact to somehow contrive a photograph. Startled, Maria ran up the stairs and I automatically followed her. We found ourselves confronted by a woman, presumably a teacher, and a sobbing Ana with one of her legs bound clumsily in a blood-stained towel. The child was distraught and ran to her mother, eyeing me with her curious little brown eyes shiny with tears. She sucked her thumb and clasped a worn toy rabbit to her face. There was a rapid exchange of Spanish. Clearly Ana had fallen over in the school playground and cut her leg. The severity of the wound was unclear, but a vociferous debate followed about the next course of action. The word 'Médico' was mentioned more than once, with a caution which implied cost.

"I can go to the pharmacy," I volunteered quickly.

The young teacher agreed readily, "Yes, that is good." She looked grateful to be handing over responsibility for the child.

I smiled at Maria, "Then Ana can stay here with you." To my surprise Ana came running over to me and gave me a hug. I knelt to face her and wiped the tears from her cheeks. I pointed at my eyes and her knee and she nodded. I slid off the make-do bandage and we all had a look. It was a graze rather than a cut, but it looked very sore with little lumps of gravel in the wound. "It just needs cleaning with hot water," I said with authority. Maria and the teacher both nodded and I headed off. Ana waved

"Bote?" I speculated. The word sounded the same in Spanish. "Does he own a boat? With a broken engine? ... moto roto ... kaput ..."

Maria laughed animatedly: "Moto roto? No! He has fishing boat." She made a gesture, like rowing, her elbows rotating.

I sighed, "But no engine? Moto?"

She shrugged: "No."

Then why would he need money for engine parts and fuel? He had no car. It didn't make sense. I mulled the questions over in my mind and watched her. Maria poured herself a generous measure of Rioja from a carafe on the table and took a sip. I didn't want her out of control in any way. I knew about Maria and red wine. One glass maybe, but two, and at this time of the morning? She replaced her glass on the table and folded her hands in her lap. She was very composed, smiling brightly at me still. I took her hand and looked her closely in the eyes:

"Maria. I must take a photograph ... Debo tomar un fotografía ..." I made a square shape with my hands and a clicking sound like a shutter ... "Of Henri ... photograph"

She shook her head but said: "Si."

I continued: "A secret photograph."

She mimicked my exact words: "A secret photograph?"

I pointed upwards to the ceiling: "Si, Maria. Henri. Secret."

"Secreto ... entiendo. Si. Yes, I understand." Her large brown eyes sparkled with an air of mischief I couldn't comprehend. I never knew what she was really thinking.

perspiring slightly. Her top lip was moist, she brushed her tongue across it in an almost childlike way. She watched my mouth as I formed the intricate Spanish words.

"Qué? ... I don't know." Her expression was blank.

I squeezed her arm. Our trusty dictionary and atlas were on the table. I tried to conjure up phrases as best I could.

"Where is he from? ... De dónde es ...? Henri?"

Maria leant over me and flicked through the atlas. I could feel her warmth, her scent; her hair brushed my arm. She found the page with the country she was looking for and her unvarnished nail found Switzerland.

"Suiza," she said softly and looked at me. "Here."

"Have you seen his identity papers? ... Documentos de identidad?" I rustled my thumb and fingers to make the sound of paper, but it was perfectly clear she understood.

Maria shook her head: "Documentos? No."

Suddenly she stood and asked me if I wanted something to drink - coffee, orange juice or water. I opted for water, which had been boiled and left to cool in large storage jars in a larder in the corner. She went over, poured me a glass, and brought it over to me. Then she came and sat beside me once again, rearranging her hair.

"Gracias, Maria ... I don't think he's Swiss ... not Suiza, no ..." I drank some water and went on to ask her – as best I could – why he would he need money for engine parts and fuel. I improvised with engine noises and exhaust, which made her

peeler, screwdriver, paintbrush – and we wrote the relevant Spanish, French and English words on the page. It was basic, but it worked. The lessons helped us all. José, never the most effervescent of characters, seemed preoccupied, and he went to sit out on the veranda, smoking and drinking as soon as he had finished his meal. Maria made herself busy with clearing away the dishes and washing up.

She had made eye contact with me many times that evening, but never with José; it was as if they were barely aware of each other. But she knew I needed to speak with her.

*

In the morning I went down to the basement kitchen having prepared a mental list of questions for Maria. She was sitting at the kitchen table and smiled brightly as I joined her. The air down here was always cool and smelt of basil, oregano, rosemary, and other herbs I couldn't identify. There was a fragrance of sweet-smelling wood polish that blended in magically with garlic and wine. Maria wore a white blouse and a pinafore, her long black hair hung freely. I touched her shoulder in greeting and began slowly.

"What is the name of the man?" I pointed upwards ... "el hombre de arriba ... neighbour?"

"Henri," she replied quietly.

"Henri what? ... Qué?"

Maria

Residencia López-Cordera, Villaricos, Spain

EARLY JUNE '45 AND ANOTHER brutally hot day in southern Spain started for me at 5am. I hadn't slept well and despite the mosquito net, a couple of the little blighters had got in and bitten me. My dreams, when I had managed to sleep, were unsettled. I was anxious to speak to Maria alone. I didn't want to involve José, and I certainly didn't want to alert my neighbour to the fact that I was on to him. He was certainly on to me. I waited until the children were both at school, José was out working, and the neighbour was absent from the villa once again. The previous evening's dinner with the Cordera family had been a lively affair. Maria had made fish stew with potatoes and peppers, which had been washed down with several glasses of Rioja.

Antonio and Ana were full of mischief, and as usual it had been my job to entertain them once we had all eaten. They wanted to learn more French and English words, so I drew a series of household objects. The lessons were becoming more

My Spanish must have impressed her: "No, gracias." She paid for the bread, and we walked together through the market. It was noisy and busy, exotic aromas pervaded the hot air.

*

From a concealed spot by the church, the neighbour witnessed the encounter, unobserved. He frowned. How much had been overheard in the post office, he wondered? And what could possibly happen next?

cashier reminded me that I was next in the queue to be served. I shook my head and went out in pursuit.

Once outside in the bright sunshine, I found that my quarry had vanished. I faced a busy market with numerous stalls selling local produce and everything from broomsticks to hats. The transition from the dull light inside the post office to bright sunlight was dazzling. I scrunched my eyes to readjust. I dashed across the plaza and sheltered under a palm tree with my heart thumping. Who was he? Who was he speaking to? He was quite obviously German, so he must be on the run. What were the options: Wehrmacht? Luftwaffe? Kriegsmarine? Even SS? If so, how could he be so far from Berlin? Surely all the SS and Gestapo had either been captured or killed by the Russians?

One thing was certain, I urgently needed to get a message back to the UK, but what actual evidence did I have? None. No, this needed careful thought and planning. I would ask Maria just how much she knew. I wouldn't confide in José; there was something about him that I didn't quite trust. At least I had a little time. But how much?

And then I spotted Maria buying bread from what looked like an old stagecoach covered with a heavy canvas awning. She wore a floppy hat, sunglasses, and a long summer dress. I waved, wandered over and said hello, she smiled and removed her sunglasses, blinking in the glare. We edged under the awning, out of the sun. I asked her if she wanted a hand with the shopping.

for a connection ... Oh, I see... yes, put me through." He fed the machine with coins, which clattered into a collection box. Then he switched to German. Quietly, with no greeting, no names exchanged. "I need money for engine parts and fuel. Wire some quickly. Yes, I am in Spain." Then he repeated the name Banco Etcheverría – a well-known Spanish bank – and quantities of American dollars and their equivalent value in pesetas. He repeated the instructions for absolute clarity and understanding of the exchange rate and process. His next words were chilling; I couldn't believe what I was hearing.

"Someone else is staying at the Residencia. A woman, on her own. I searched her room and found her French ID. Hidden in a drawer. The old strand-of-hair trick for concealment. What is she doing here? She must be a spy. Maybe ex-Resistance. Even SOE. Who knows.? I should kill her, but I can't take the risk of being caught and arrested. I must get out of Spain and there are others coming."

My heart sank, I felt physically sick. There was a break and I strained to listen to the person on the other end. It was impossible. There was another break as the person at the end of the line responded. Then the stranger said firmly:

"The money, as quick as you can." He hung up abruptly. I didn't have to see him to know that it was the voice of my neighbour, but I stole a cautious glance as he turned and left the booth. Loden hat, determined pace, a certain swagger in his gait. Just as he approached the exit of the building, his step faltered. I

villa. There were no locks on doors; it wasn't that type of household, but I was confident that they respected my privacy.

The next morning after breakfast, I mentioned it to Maria. We were alone in the villa: José was on a hunting expedition with some locals, Antonio and Ana were at school, the neighbour was absent as usual. Her expression darkened as I explained what I had found. I spoke very slowly and clearly in English, and she understood what I was asking her

"No," she said with a trace of hurt in her large brown eyes: "I not touch your things – I clean room and change sheets. And towels." She glanced down at the floor like a chastised child and I felt sorry for what seemed like an accusation. Or a reprimand.

I said I was sorry again and she turned and left the kitchen. I had clearly upset her, and I certainly hadn't intended to.

*

A short time later, I was at the post office in the Plaza de la Constitución waiting in a queue to get some change to make my ritual call to the Bar-Tabac near Tarbes. I needed to speak to Michel. Alongside the counter were two wooden telephone booths; they were enclosed on three sides, but the fourth side was open to the room. I could hear an agitated man speaking to the telephone operator in broken Spanish. It sounded nothing like the local dialect the Cordera family spoke. This was a foreigner making a clumsy effort. He didn't shout, but his tone

sharpener – my days of whittling with a blunt knife were long gone. The pencils were perfectly aligned. Normally. It was the fact my pencils were slightly askew which alerted me to an intrusion into my apartment.

I quickly found my CNI, which I had concealed in the back of a stout copy of the Bible found at the bottom of the chest of drawers below the shuttered window. I had replaced it where I'd found it, nestling among folded cotton sheets and pillowcases. There was a strong smell of camphor from a cluster of mothballs. My card had not been tampered with – the strand of hair - tucked behind it - was as I had left it.

The card identified me as Claude Moreau and recorded my sex, height, colour of eyes, date and place of birth and the post office in Paris where it had been issued and stamped. My home address was stated as 23b rue Ramey, Clignancourt. The black and white photograph of me had been taken in a studio in London, not in Paris, but it was a perfect forgery. There was no trace of the Englishwoman known as Lucy Fry; nobody knew my true identity. Even the gum used to stick the photograph to the card had been manufactured in France.

It was a relief that the card hadn't been found, but the fact remained that my things had been tampered with. Nothing had been stolen, but there wasn't really anything worth stealing apart from the camera, and that would have been hard to sell in such a small community. The pencils were out of alignment because someone had flicked through the pages of my sketch pads. I

performing a wonderful Flamenco dance after she had indulged in a few glasses of Vino Tinto. Her chin jutted haughtily as, hands on hips and eyes smouldering, she tapped on the wooden floor. She came alive; it was incredibly sensual to watch. We clapped in time to the escalating rhythm of her performance. Maria emanated a beguiling feminine sexuality.

Still the neighbour upstairs said nothing and didn't participate in the family's fun and games. We didn't see him for days, but I didn't ask questions. Strangely, he was never even referred to by José and Maria. I wondered if they had conversations with him about me. I doubted it. My neighbour was a silent enigma. Sometimes during his unexplained absences, I wondered if he was a figment of my imagination. But then he would return and sit on the veranda in silence until darkness fell.

I am, by nature, tidy and well-organised. Each of my modest possessions had its place. In the tiny bathroom, my toothbrush and paste stood on a glass shelf above the washbasin with my hairbrush and comb. The bed was just a mattress, and above it a mosquito net was suspended, with weights at each corner, operated by a simple rope-and-pulley system. Each evening I had to lower the net like a huge tea cosy to completely envelop the bed and then duck quickly underneath it. Even with this precaution, a few of the cunning little devils found their way in. On a small table beside the bed were the other contents of my case: the Georges Simenon novel Freddie had given me, my

of origin: a precaution I found particularly unnerving, because I had done the same thing with mine. He didn't want to be identified, and neither did I.

I hadn't met anyone in Villaricos who could converse in English or French, and I was determined to increase my Spanish vocabulary. Early one afternoon, in the heat of the sun, I went to the cool of the local library and found an illustrated English-Spanish dictionary which I studied in the evenings in my room. Nobody in the family knew why I was there, who I was or what I was doing in Spain. Maria didn't even ask for any identification after I handed her some of the pesetas which Michel had given me. Part of the deal was that, in lieu of rent, I would help teach the children a little English and French.

After dinner I would sit with Maria and the children and teach them using drawings and simple words. We began with the necessities: please, thank you, hello, and goodbye. We moved on to everyday nouns like wine, bread, fish, meat and water. As the hot summer continued, Maria and the children added to their store of words in both English and French. The purchase of an atlas had improved their geography. Maria was naturally smart. She had a raw intelligence that was probably fueled by her instinct for survival. In the first year she had learned to understand and speak a great deal of English. She was complex and, I was to discover, entirely unpredictable.

Sometimes in the warm evenings, particularly at weekends, we sang Spanish folk songs by candlelight. This time it was my

and pretty; her husband was probably in his mid-thirties and old beyond his years, his deeply lined skin tanned from years at sea. He was surly and preoccupied, a man with troubles. On closer inspection, one noticed the scars of burns around his hairline and ears. He had clearly been through something, but what? An accident? A fire? Something traumatic anyway.

I had telephoned the Bar-Tabac near Tarbes many times, expecting news of some sort. But there had never been a message for me from Michel or from any other member of the SCIENTIST Network. Although it was disappointing, I knew there was still a possibility that a wounded serviceman would need my knowledge of the terrain.

The man who was to become my next-door neighbour at the Residencia arrived at dawn one day in the middle of June. I was sitting on the balcony, unable to sleep, when I saw José coming silently out to meet him in the road. The stranger was a man of about forty-five, under six feet tall, fair-haired and of normal build. My SOE training dictated that I took in every detail as if it mattered. Over time, after he moved in, I tried to engage him in conversation, always to no avail. He began to fascinate me. I noticed he always wore a Loden hat, a style I knew was popular in Germany for fishing and shooting. Its peak provided protection from the sun, covering part of his face. His taciturn manner towards me bordered on rudeness. We shared verandas, and I had checked the laundry he had left hanging on the clothesline one day when I knew he was out fishing in a hired

geography. 'Always be prepared to run,' Sykes at Arisaig House had told me. 'You'll never know when you might have to.'

The terrain around Villaricos was desert: Sierra Alhamilla and Los Filabres. To the west, towards Granada, the plains of the Sierra Nevada resembled Mexico: a rough, arid and ancient land with red, purple and brown contours scorched by the sun. Night would be the only sensible time to attempt to travel any distance through that landscape and even then, the horses would soon become exhausted as the barren land bled out the enormous heat it had absorbed during the day.

My apartment at the top of the villa had a view of the coast and part of a quay where small fishing boats bobbed at anchor. The pink stucco two-storey residence had been built in the Andalusian style. The design was clearly influenced by Moorish architecture: its archways, doorways and windows had a characteristic look of North Africa. The Moors had occupied Spain for several centuries, and reminders of their presence were everywhere. The sound of crickets at night was omnipresent, as were the fragrant scents of orange and bougainvillea. I slept on a mattress on the floor which was protected to some extent by a mosquito net. I could hear the high-pitched squeal of mosquitoes baying for blood on the other side of the mesh as I lay in search of sleep. Finally, at around 3am, I would drop off as the heat in the room decreased.

Below me, the villa was occupied by the Spanish family who owned it: José and Maria Cordera and their two young children,

Apartamento

Residencia López-Cordera, Villaricos, Spain.

THE WAR HAD BEEN OVER for a month and I was living in an apartment in Villaricos, a picturesque fishing village beside the Mediterranean, where I had been working as a nanny for just over a year. There was no breeze, and time seemed to stand still. The summer heat was stifling – more than ninety degrees Fahrenheit – and fiercely oppressive. I hadn't got used to it. Early afternoons were unbearable, particularly if you had the misfortune to be exposed to the sun for any length of time. My neck and shoulders were the worst, followed by the tops of my feet.

When I first arrived in the village, I had seen an advertisement in the local shop for an apartment available for rent. The woman behind the counter had no problem understanding me and what I was looking for in terms of accommodation. She gave me the address, and I soon found Residencia López-Cordera. I knew from training the importance

Cartagena? From there to, where, North Africa?"

"Speculation?" asked Miles Villiers politely. He was a rugged, strongly built man of about forty. His sand-coloured hair was cut neatly, but not in a military style. He wouldn't have looked out of place on a rugby field or in a boxing ring. He was clearly the product of a top public school, then Oxford or Cambridge, and not a man to be trifled with. Despite his build, he spoke softly, with the air and conviction of a lawyer. Penfold's wife once remarked that Villiers was a bull in a silk suit.

"Information," said Penfold with a crafty smile. "Müller has clearly run out of money. The Vatican notes he was given in Rome have no value outside Italy. Lire aren't much better."

Villiers couldn't hide his own smile. "He can't risk another robbery in France, and he certainly can't risk killing another French citizen. So, maybe you're right, Colonel Penfold – Spain."

"Got any evidence?" asked Pritchard. His eyes landed on General Zhukov, an implacable Muscovite with no sense of humour whatsoever.

"No. But I'm inclined to the view that luck plays a vital role in the Intelligence world," said Penfold, reaching for his pipe. "Damn. It's gone out again. Where did I put my matches?" Villiers eyed Penfold carefully, sensing that something was in the air.

Villiers interjected and spoke plainly. "We want him particularly in connection with the Stalag Luft III murders. Mass-murders, if one is to be accurate."

Pritchard was chomping at the bit, jaw muscles clenching. "Well, we want him, period." He addressed the room, and everybody nodded because everybody wanted Müller. Too many of the Nazi elite had vanished.

One of the Red Army generals suddenly spoke in serviceable English. "Our information is he was given safe-haven – in the Vatican. How he got there from the embers of the Reich Chancellery is of no consequence. Some say on a white horse. Ha! The fact is, he got there. That is all."

Penfold reached for his pipe, and then thought better of it. "Yes. Our estimation is that he sailed to Corsica and then Marseille. An SOE agent in Arles was certainly killed by Müller, but not before she had the time and wisdom to file a detailed report to our friends in Paris. The agent also stated that he had killed a woman called Sophie Vidal – a waitress in Arles. Stole her life savings and robbed the till of the hotel where he was staying. The police were called, but he was long gone. That man was almost certainly Heinrich Müller. Of course, nobody knew that, including this poor Sophie character."

"So, you lost him?" said Pritchard loudly, emphasising the 'you' as if Penfold should be held personally responsible. Pritchard looked around the room; nobody reacted.

Penfold chose to ignore the dig and press on. "British

spoke with a strong Texan accent. He too had both military and civilian staff in his considerable entourage. The final figure in the room was Miles Villiers from the RAF Special Investigation Branch – SIB/North/Cranwell. Nothing proclaimed his rank, and he wore civilian clothes and didn't smoke. Every other officer was dressed in full uniform, but nobody doubted his credentials.

Penfold placed his pipe down in a glass ashtray and twitched his nose like a curious hamster as he studied some army documents marked CLASSIFIED in red ink. "What do we know about Heinrich Müller?" asked Penfold. He spoke in a clipped, upper-class accent which suited his appearance perfectly.

"Hell! 'Gestapo' Müller. Born 28 April 1900, Munich," bellowed General Pritchard with unrefined authority. "It's in the file y'all have. Great career: Munich Police, then Gestapo. Responsible for the death camps here in Germany and the East. Quite a CV for an arrogant little Jew-hater country boy."

"Yes," agreed Penfold with a sigh of impatience. "I was being rhetorical. I mean, what do we actually know? It doesn't require an answer." Penfold waited to test the water and continued.

"He was officially last seen at the Führerbunker on 1 May 1945. We are sure he escaped the day after Hitler's suicide. There were witnesses. He isn't accounted for anywhere and there is no body ... unless the Americans have him." He allowed himself the merest hint of a smile and continued, "He is the most wanted war criminal in the world. Where can he be? He must be

Penfold

Post war Army billet. British Occupied Zone, Germany.

COLONEL JOHN PENFOLD FIDDLED with his pipe until he finally got it going to the relief of the other men gathered in the room. Penfold resembled Field Marshal Montgomery so closely that it had often been postulated that he could act as a stand-in for him at public events in the interests of military security. If Winston Churchill had a double, why not Monty? The men were seated in a British Army billet. Penfold had been present when General Stumpff, Field Marshal Keitel and Admiral von Friedeburg signed the final German surrender at Karlshorst on 9 May, just over a week after Hitler's suicide in the Führerbunker under Berlin. The bunker interested Penfold, and for good reason. He eyed the other men in the room as he puffed on his ancient briar.

General Zhukov of the Red Army had three translators, and a secretary who took notes in rapid shorthand. General Pritchard

GESTAPO. She opened the folder carefully and inside was a single sheet of Nazi headed stationery and the address: Prinz-Albrecht Strasse 8, Berlin.

Typed on the page was a list of German surnames and their rank in the Third Reich. The words - or their significance - meant absolutely nothing to her.

"What are you doing?" Henri's voice asked suddenly, out of the blue. She froze, catatonic with fright. He walked over to her, and she let go of the page. He stroked her cheek gently; this was always the prelude to sex. She relaxed slightly. The Nazi document floated innocently down onto the carpet.

"It is of no consequence," he said to her, and started to casually unbutton his shirt. Sophie knew the routine, so she turned to the bed to slip off her skirt and petticoat. The last thing she saw was the grey Gestapo folder. Henri crushed her skull from behind with the base of a solid wooden table lamp, and she fell to the bed. He watched her twitch and die. He checked her radial pulse and smiled; Sophie wasn't his first kill. There had been thousands of other innocent victims. And his name wasn't Henri.

But it was close enough to Heinrich.

part of a book-signing tour. La Maison Jaune – the yellow house – was an 1888 oil on canvas by Dutch painter Vincent van Gogh. And so, the venue was deemed appropriate. Although the actual building van Gogh had rented back then was 2 Place Lamartine in Arles, it had been severely damaged in a bombing raid by the Allies – a year before - on June 25, 1944.

Raimbault and Pourcel, two flamboyant Parisian luminaries had been forced into hiding during Nazi occupation. But now, in peace time, as minor celebrities, they were surrounded by eager journalists, newspaper photographers and general hangers on. Pourcel's recently published book about the life and work of van Gogh had caused quite a stir among literary circles.

The bulbs of a dozen cameras flashed and momentarily illuminated their boyish good looks and raffish clothes. A cameraman from Le Figaro took a significant photograph of the lively event. Sophie was fascinated as the colourful pair drank in the attention as they posed for photographs.

Henri remained on the fringes and watched with contempt. He disapproved of such bourgeois exhibitionism and, when he'd had enough, disappeared from the courtyard, and didn't return that night.

The following afternoon, Sophie's eyes were drawn to Henri's small suitcase, which stood in the corner of her room. She looked out of the window, there was no sign of Henri or Valois, and curiosity got the better of her. She picked up the case, placed it on her bed and opened it apprehensively. Beneath Henri's shirts,

where Sophie was drying glasses and talking to customers. She must have looked particularly pretty that day, with her hair pinned up and minimal makeup. She wore a long summer dress that emphasized the contours of her figure. After a week or so Henri invited her for tea and cakes by the cathedral. He told her he was Swiss – from Basle – and had spent weeks hiding from the Germans. His French was not good - but they muddled along – she had picked up some German in those challenging war years, enough to communicate.

Every day for a week he brought her flowers and trinkets: nothing of value, but she appreciated the thought. Sophie came to like this mystery man from Switzerland. He told her he cared for her. Henri said he was forty-five, unmarried and a schoolteacher. After several weeks, he had moved into her tiny room at the back of the hotel. But behind the scenes Henri paid Valois a substantial sum to cover domestic expenses such as electricity and food. But in the end Valois was a common souteneur and Sophie was the innocent victim of greed. Their love affair was a callous scam which Sophie believed was real. On her days off she took him to see some of the famous Roman landmarks. When she was working, he would disappear and return late, and she never questioned him about where he had been or what he had been doing. He was a puzzle.

*

needed a waitress, and he knew the value of a pretty face. Bernard Valois was inscrutable and knew which side his bread was buttered.

Her new job changed her life. Sophie began to be noticed, by guests at the hotel, and by the pilgrims who came to visit the site of van Gogh's former home. Valois had been right in his judgement that he would have an asset in his attractive niece. Far from being avuncular, he was an arrogant, self-serving manipulator of women and, despite his manner, he was surprisingly successful with them. He tried to manipulate Sophie, but he couldn't.

The hotel attracted a range of clients: businesspeople, travelling salesmen, bankers with expense accounts – men with money. Uncle Bernard was totally unselfish, he tried to negotiate on Sophie's behalf, but as a good Catholic girl she would not sell herself, even though the money was sometimes tempting. For seven years – and throughout the German occupation – she remained at the hotel, working hard and resisting all the temptations put before her.

Valois and his bawdy cronies at the bar would chide her through clouds of tobacco smoke for her stubbornness. "You're sitting on a fortune. Take it while you can," they would say, laughing at her primness. The implication was that her looks wouldn't last forever.

"I may be stubborn, but at least I'm free," she would reply with one eyebrow arched.

Sophie

Fourteen months later; after the German surrender 7th May 1945.

Hôtel la Maison Jaune, Arles, France.

SOPHIE VIDAL WAS TWENTY-FIVE but looked older. She was striking in a Garboesque way, with an ethereal quality which made her seem vulnerable, almost fragile. It was her eyes, of course. Her aloof, standoffish attitude made her even more appealing. Her admirers wanted to discover her; to know the woman behind the elusive facade.

She was born in 1920 in Arles, a town in the Bouches-du Rhône département in southern France. She'd left school when she was fourteen and worked in the vineyards, like so many of her contemporaries. It was tough work for a young girl, but there was little choice. Money was scarce, opportunities limited. However, when she was eighteen, fortune intervened, and she secured a job as a waitress in a hotel near the Roman

of the sparkling blue Mediterranean was hard to resist, and I had made it this far.

I still had a few cherished possessions in my case; my camera and drawing utensils. And the Georges Simenon novel from Brim that Freddie had given me at Beaulieu. The memory made me silently chuckle and I clutched the case closely for comfort. I had a stout bundle of pesetas in there too, certainly sufficient for a year. I would just have to find a paying job to get by and make my presence credible. I also had the phone number of the Bar-Tabac Michel and I had visited just outside Tarbes. I could contact him there if the need arose or to check for any instructions from London. He and I had studied a map of southern Spain and decided that the town of Villaricos seemed a good place to hide out. It was the right size. I should be able to live there inconspicuously and have an indirect telephone lifeline to Brim. Life could be a lot worse.

frontier where, by village custom, several dozen French and Spanish people gossiped for a couple of hours every Sunday afternoon. There were children, flowers, laughter and general merriment. When people began to drift away my guide transferred me to another 'cut-out', a tall Spaniard introduced as Miguel, although it was understood that nobody was using their real name. He was my escort for the next stage of the journey through Puigcerda to Barcelona.

Although that VIC line had been compromised in October 1942, Miguel insisted it was safe enough for me, and I had to trust his judgement on this. I looked the part with a headscarf over my hair, my peasant clothes were suitably torn and dusty, and my Spanish was adequate. However, once I was in Spain, I knew I was far from freedom. Any agent was painfully aware that, if they fell foul of Franco's police, they might end up spending many months in the clamour of the camp at Miranda de Ebro, or somewhere equally unpleasant, even if they might eventually manage to obtain a false identity from the British Consulate.

Michel Basin had provided me with papers describing me as a Sister of the Sanctuary of our Lady of Lourdes, the Catholic shrine. This identity at least allowed me to say very little. I parted company with Miguel and boarded a 20-seater bus at Badalona, and the next stage of my journey began. The other passengers were all Spanish: several women, workmen, and a couple of sailors who had been paid off in Barcelona. The bus

and I were peeling apples. I could see he had something on his mind:

"Pierre received a message from London. You are to travel to southern Spain and stay there. Be prepared to assist SOE agents or downed RAF pilots in getting to Gibraltar. I will give you a telephone number to call once a week. I have also been instructed to give you plenty of cash to cover your expenses."

My heart sank. That was not what I had hoped to hear; I just wanted to go home. Michel could see I was disappointed and continued, "It's not the end of the world, there are some beautiful seaside towns west of Cartagena, down to Villaricos and beyond. Think of it as a holiday."

Michel was right of course; this was an opportunity. Much as I desired to go back to England, I had a responsibility to carry on. Not only for Brim and the Service, but also for Freddie who was always at the back of my mind. His face and gentle eyes encouraging and spurring me on. Over the next few days, I bought new clothes. The network created travel passes and papers to establish my credibility and get me across the border. Chantal helped me to brush up on my Spanish and coached me on the local culture and history. After Bordeaux and the weeks of preparation here in Tarbes, I was glad to be moving on. The best of the escape lines established by DF Section did not involve much strenuous walking.

My initial guide ran most of VIC's crossings from Perpignan, where the mountains are reasonably low and easy to negotiate.

teacher. (I have left SCIENTIST – my assignment) – implying there was a problem. I ended: and now I will roam, in search of your love. (I await instructions from you.)

The poem system was complicated, and it took me over ten minutes to convert my plaintext into code. Now came the risky bit of the procedure. Pierre had to tap out the double-bluff message in Morse code as quickly as possible before the Germans had the opportunity to detect his transmission and trace its source. The B2 had been switched to battery power, which made it harder to trace. After transmission, in accordance with a strict instruction from Leo, I set light to the strip of the silk sheet on which the recognition code had been printed. The evidence now no longer existed.

On the journey back home, Michel insisted on calling into a Bar-Tabac, just outside Tarbes. The owner of the bar clearly knew him well, as did most of the customers. He quickly sank two large cognacs and smoked a few cigarettes. For the first time in more than an hour, he relaxed. He held up the packet of Gitanes and said:

"Don't tell Chantal, eh?"

I shook my head and smiled. "You are fond of Pierre, I can see. He is important to you and you did not like placing him at risk by transmitting to England."

"He is my cousin, you know. His wife left him and took everything, including his two daughters and most of his money. Yes, we are fond of Pierre. Someone has to be." He flashed a

Major Charles Pelham and his tall, gangly frame.

I dug into my bag and unscrewed the mirrored top half of a round metal makeup compact. The rifling – helical grooved patterns machined into the internal surface of the compact – formed an airtight seal with the top. I retrieved a carefully compressed square sheet of white silk which unfolded to the size of a pocket hanky. The silk was covered with strips: lines of photographed numbers printed onto the silk. Thank you, Leo Marks, SOE.

The two men looked at it, intrigued. "What's this?" asked Pierre with growing interest.

"A new method of coding messages. Unbreakable." I handled the delicate silk with care. It had been hidden in the secret compartment for months, but it was safe and intact, and unfolded without a crease. It was a Letter One-Time Pad (LOP), a method devised to prevent the Germans from decoding SOE messages. The procedure employed a complex numerical coding system with a unique key for each message. The only other copy of the pad was as at Poundon. The gatekeepers were Pelham and Leo Marks.

I began my message with the secret numerical sequence which identified me as Scorpius:19-3-15-18-16-9-21-19. Next came a set of numerals which indicated which number-pad I was using. I had decided to use the 'Playfair' method, based on a line of a poem which Leo had devised specially for me. It would be clear to the decoder at Poundon that the message was genuine,

We drew up outside a grand old farmhouse which had seen better days. The door opened, and a man of about forty came out to greet us. He was short and swarthy and, like many people at that time, looked distinctly undernourished.

"No names," said Michel as we climbed out of the beaten-up old car. It too had seen better days, but it was clearly his pride and joy.

"But I know his," I said with a trace of insolence I immediately regretted.

"He doesn't know yours," countered Michel. "He doesn't know who you are, what you are or where you are from. And that will become important if he is captured by the Germans." There was a vague shake of his head.

"In any case, Pierre isn't his real name."

"Can he be trusted?" I persisted, but I just had to know.

"Pierre is loyal. That's all you need to know."

We entered a spacious kitchen with a flagstone floor, a low ceiling and a very large solid-looking wooden table. No words had been exchanged at all, just initial nods of introduction. On the table was a familiar B2 transceiver. It had probably been parachute-dropped by an SOE-seconded Lysander into a field, or possibly the sea. The set came in a case with four compartments. The left side was for accessories: a Morse key, headphones, an aerial, and an antenna with an 18-metre cable. This now trailed out of the kitchen through an open window and up into a tree. The B2 could be run from mains electricity or a battery. This set

uncharacteristically distracted mood: preoccupied, I realised later, with getting me out of his life. They had given me haven, but I was a burden to the Basins, and I was putting them in danger. I couldn't blame them for being eager to move me on. At some stage we turned off the main road in the direction of a forest, on a rough track which challenged the old Renault's fragile suspension. I glanced over to my left at Michel's furrowed brow.

"Where are we going?" I asked guardedly. Although I trusted both Michel and his wife implicitly, there was always that margin of caution. It was unavoidable, continually living on the edge and always being on guard.

"To the Radio-Operator's house. His name is Pierre, and it is not far."

"Good, thank you." I glanced across at him. He was clenching the wheel like a man possessed.

"Keep it as short as possible. The German radio counter-intelligence scan the airwaves constantly, listening for unexpected enemy signals. They can cross-coordinate and get a location in minutes. It wouldn't take the crafty bastards long to find us. And if they did, they'd kill us all, after a lengthy interrogation."

I sighed. I knew Michel wasn't exaggerating the delicacy of the situation. I rummaged around in my handbag and felt the contours of what I knew I would need for the transmission to Poundon.

Mercedes.

The streets were far from safe when I first arrived in Tarbes and sought out my contact. There was an omnipresent fear, not only of the Waffen SS Panzer Divisions, but also of Nazi collaborators and informers. Michel had been understandably suspicious, but eventually he agreed to help me. All I had to substantiate my story was my forged CNI which bore my photograph and an address in Paris which he may have known as a safe house. More important to gaining his trust was my detailed knowledge. Most of the SOE agents parachuted into Occupied France were expected; I had simply arrived out of the blue with no prior warning. He asked me a series of complex questions, all of which I had been told to expect by my trainers at Group B finishing school at Beaulieu. And of course, Freddie's questions in the back of the Alvis that day in the New Forest.

Michel knew from his network about Commander Heller's fate in Bordeaux. It wasn't public knowledge because the news would have been bad for German morale: the Kriegsmarine were sensitive souls. Michel and his wife Chantal, also a member of the Resistance, took me into their farmhouse home and prepared me for the journey. I had no idea where I was going, but I knew I had to escape from France.

I was anxious to get a message back to England and explained to Michel the importance of sending a signal. My last had been sent from the SCIENTIST network in Bordeaux ten days before. The following morning, Michel and I drove out of

Lucy

Tarbes Safe House, France.

MARCH 1944 AND MY JOURNEY FROM TARBES in France down to the Spanish Frontier was long and tortuous, and I couldn't have done it without the courageous aid of the French Resistance and the DF (SOE Escape Section) – the VIC line. The route over the Pyrenees was an old and established smugglers' trail which they knew well. I was following in the footsteps of many esteemed predecessors: FANYs such as Giliana Gerson, Virginia Hall and Odette Wilen. They had all got out by the same route. There were similar escape routes all over France.

In addition to his role in the Resistance, Michel Basin worked at the Morane-Saulnier Aircraft factory at Tarbes where the Dewoitine D.520 fighters were built. Michel was a test pilot connected to the 1er groupe de chasse 'Doret', a unit established by the Resistance forces of the interior (FFI), originally from the Toulouse area. The only information I had been given by SOE in Baker Street was Michel's name and where he could be found. It

a cigarette. The thought of being stranded, alone in a foreign country, terrified her. Whoever Scorpius was, they were bloody brave.

Pelham nodded at Barbara and laid the cue down carefully on the main communal desk. It was covered with maps, charts and signals. The operator responded after three rings.

"Yes, hello," Pelham said, "put me through to Professor Brimblecombe's office, please." There was a pause as the operator tried to locate the professor, who could be at one of any number of MI6 facilities around London and the Home Counties. Pelham looked at Barbara impatiently as he gripped the handset.

He spoke firmly as the operator replied. "Yes, it is urgent. Damned urgent."

WHEELWRIGHT network. It was tapped out as 19-3-15-18-16-9-21-19."

"Scorpius," said Pelham.

"Does it mean something, sir?"

"Perhaps," said Pelham with alarm. Of course, he knew of Scorpius. The Artist, who was in deep cover. He had met her twice at informal meetings with Brim and knew she was highly regarded by British Intelligence and MI6 top brass.

Barbara continued, "'Eyes only' encryption, sir. Playfair. One for you and Mr. Marks." She looked at Pelham, knowing the gravity of the situation.

He nodded. So, Scorpius was in France, and in danger. The other reason for such a signal was to confirm that the agent was, at least, alive. But Pelham's colleagues would want to know the full story, and they must be told immediately.

"I'll get on to it at once." She might have been captured, Pelham speculated, and somehow escaped. Now she could be on the run, pursued by the enemy. "Anything else?" asked Pelham anxiously. He bit his lip.

"No. WHEELWRIGHT is Tarbes, I believe. That was all, sir."

Pelham walked swiftly over to a large wall map of Europe and picked up a snooker cue which he liked to use as a pointer. "Tarbes is here," he said, tapping a spot in the Occupied Zone thoughtfully. He picked up the telephone and quickly dialled an internal number. Whoever sent that communication was taking a hell of a risk.

admitted to the base with a salute, and he wheeled his bike into a parade ground-sized courtyard surrounded by a cluster of single-storey buildings. A tall radio mast towered among them, supported by steel guy wires and protected by barbed-wire fencing. A couple of infantrymen stood on guard duty somewhat languidly, but soon adjusted their posture when they caught sight of Pelham's commanding figure.

The Station was Pelham's personal fiefdom: a half-timbered building painted in camouflage green-grey with blacked-out windows. He slotted his front wheel into a bicycle rack next to several other aged machines.

Once inside, Pelham was greeted by Barbara, an attractive twenty-four-year-old uniformed Wren, who was standing under an electric light in a haze of tobacco smoke. There were about fifteen people on duty in the hut, each sitting at a desk with an Anglepoise lamp. Some wore headsets. There was a constant and unforgiving noise in the room from the clatter of teleprinters and typewriters, the sound of telephones and the buzz of an ancillary generator, all punctuated by shouts of elation and dismay. It was a frenetic hive of activity seven days a week.

Barbara spoke in what she had described in her interview as a 'very slight Oxfordshire country accent.' Today she looked uncommonly serious; she held a sheet of paper in her hand and tapped her chin with a neatly sharpened pencil. She waited until Pelham had taken his coat off and removed his bicycle clips before she caught his attention. He listened carefully to what she

Poundon

FCO/MI6 Intelligence HQ, Poundon, Buckinghamshire, England.

AS USUAL, Major Charles Pelham left home with time to spare. His shift didn't begin until 7am, but he was habitually punctual. After a cup of weak tea he pecked his wife Carole on the cheek and said goodbye. She stood at the front door and watched him cycle up the road, his long, gangly legs pumping like pistons; coat tails flapping in the wind. He pedalled quickly from their ivy-clad cottage in the Buckinghamshire village of Steeple Claydon and towards what staff referred to as 'the base.'

FCO/MI6 Signals Intelligence at Poundon Hill was about four miles away from home, and the ride always did Pelham good. It woke him up and set his mind in focus for whatever lay ahead that day – every day was different. He arrived at the gatehouse breathless, but not over-exerted.

Pelham was a tall, slim man in his mid-thirties. His wife worried that he worked too hard, but signals, ciphers and

name, and she knew where the Resistance network was located; that was all. She retrieved Heller's car key from the jacket pocket of his Kriegsmarine uniform and inspected it carefully. It was for a Mercedes Type G4 Staff Car. Dammit! –the bloody thing would stick out like a sore thumb. The gleaming black machine was decked out with Swastika and Reich eagle flags along each front wing. The headlamps were like two gleaming dinner plates. She might as well have a fanfare to announce her escape. At least there wasn't a driver waiting. Christ! – this wasn't written in the rulebook. But then she remembered Brim telling her: there wasn't a rulebook. As always, it was all she had. She would have to make do. She closed her eyes and visualised a map of France. Go! was all she could think. Lucy Fry was on the run. And on her own.

groin, exactly where she had been told to. The bullet pierced his femoral artery. A perfect hit. His white underwear immediately exploded with blood. The look on his face was incredulous as he slumped headfirst onto the bed. Heller tried to speak, but no words were forthcoming. A moment later there was a knock on the bedroom door and a woman asking her if everything was all right. She wasn't – she felt sick - but tried desperately to compose herself.

"Everything's fine! Yes, thank you! It was just a bottle of champagne! It's my birthday! Thank you, Madame."

Presumably satisfied that all that she had heard was the report of a champagne cork, the woman retired. Claude got out of bed – fully dressed – to open the window. The room stank of gunpowder and there were tendrils of smoke hanging in the air. She unwrapped the Luger and cleaned it with the towel, eradicating her prints thoroughly. Then she placed the handgrip of the gun into the stiffening fingers of Commander Heller, trying to look neither at his face nor the horrible wound.

She glanced down at Heller's leg. Strapped to his calf was a leather sheath containing a stiletto. So, he had intended to kill her anyway. This was to be their last night. Had he discovered she was a spy, or was he just being careful? Immediately her mind flicked to the faces of the members of her network in Bassens. Had she been betrayed? Surely not.

Hurriedly she found her suitcase under the bed and prepared to leave. Now that she knew what Heller had intended, she didn't

"What of it?" Heller sounded suspicious for the first time in their affair.

"I–I was just amazed it had enough petrol, that's all. America is a long way."

"Diesel," said Heller. "She ran on diesel."

She laughed, trying to dismiss the implied threat. "I've run out of petrol driving from here to the warehouse in Langon. Maybe the U-Boat had spare tanks. Or a very long range?"

"But why do you want to know? Why is it of interest?" He moved closer to her; the sexual flame was flickering now. Nearly extinguished.

"Curiosity," the young woman said, and it almost sounded convincing.

"You've been very curious about a lot of things recently, Claude. Especially U-Boats. Why?"

"You are a U-Boat Commander; I am just trying to show an interest in your work."

"I am not the commander of U123." He moved closer to the bed, and she immediately sensed danger. He had changed. This was not the romantic Lothario; this was someone else.

"Drink some wine, Dieter, then come and kiss me. I need some love."

He reached down as if to remove a sock. And then his tone changed back again. "All right," he said with a sudden charming smile. "Let's go to it."

She whispered seductively, "No Dieter, let's not."

Médoc, Fronsac, Pomerol and other wine areas of Bordeaux. The knowledgeable young woman would necessarily accompany him, and she soon discovered that his penchant for fine French red wine was as healthy as his appetite for sex.

"... And then, of course, there is the crossing from Rostock in Northern Germany to Gedser in Storstrom, Denmark," Heller continued. "All these islands are perfect for sailing. My brother and I spent many summers there on our father's yacht – of course, Karl is younger than I. It is he in that family photograph I showed you, on board the motor vessel Heidelberg."

She remembered the picture of Karl Heller and pretended to listen with great interest as his brother carefully poured two glasses of the classic Bordeaux and passed her one. She had gone to a great deal of trouble to procure this rare wine from a supplier in Blaye. She put the glass down, untouched, on the bedside table as he finally hung up the last of his uniform and closed the doors of the armoire. He picked up her lace panties from the bed and brushed them against his lips. Then he seemed to change his mind as a thought occurred to him. "By the way, I have been thinking. Why did you ask me about U-Boat 123 the other night? It is out of character for a young woman like you to have any interest in the German navy." He looked hard at her face.

"Isn't that the one that sailed all the way to America and back?" She spoke abstractedly, as if she wasn't really sure and didn't particularly care about the German U-Boat which had

finest private schools and lived in a villa on Wannsee with their parents. Their father was a lawyer, their mother a paediatrician. They had staff: cooks, nannies, gardeners, chauffeurs and personal secretaries. The Heller family enjoyed the best that life had to offer.

Dieter began his Reichsmarine career in 1927 and was very quickly promoted. He was awarded the Oak Leaves to his Knight's Cross in June 1941. The presentation was made by Adolf Hitler at the Führer HQ at the Wolfsschanze in Rastenburg. It was, Heller had said, the proudest moment of his life. The award was made in recognition of the sinking of 34 British and American ships in the North Atlantic; 187,267 tons all told, and thousands of lives lost. The nightly attacks against Allied convoys had been all about formation and timing; a rapid launch of lethal torpedoes against unsuspecting destroyers and frigates causing massive loss, designed to starve Britain into submission. Commander Heller was a hero of the Third Reich, and consequently a target for assassination, but that possibility seemed to have eluded both the Abwehr and the Nazi High Command.

Heller was an extraordinarily attractive man; charming and intelligent. His weaknesses were wine and sex. And plenty of both. Claude, of course, knew this. She had pursued Heller with care and meticulous planning, catching his eye from behind the counter of the wine shop and allowing him to woo her for more than three months before capitulating. She was well aware that,

with velvet head and footboards. Her head was propped up against two plump pillows, and she gave the impression she was naked beneath the sheets: naked and ready – thrilling to the eye. She watched the man undress, slowly and meticulously folding his clothes and placing them in the spacious armoire. He hung his Kriegsmarine uniform on a wooden hanger, continuing to talk enthusiastically about the life of a mariner and the challenges of navigating the Baltic in a storm.

The bedroom was French in style and decoration – too floral and fussy for the man's Germanic taste, but it had served a purpose. He was excited at the prospect of what he thought was about to come. Vivid images flashed through his mind, and he smiled at the prospect of making love to her one last time. She manifested sensuality, and her uninhibited passion was addictive. Her hips and thighs were shapely, her breasts firm and round.

He noticed an uncorked bottle of Château Lafite Rothschild 1936 and two large glasses on a table. She was a marvellous lover; she thought of everything. Her lingerie was scattered on top of the bed, except for her silk stockings. He swallowed in anticipation. Another perfect night of passion and fine wine while his crew were all in the mess playing cards and drinking cheap French beer. Too bad; these were the benefits of rank and authority. He would enjoy this evening's swansong with relish.

Commander Dieter Heller had a lot to be grateful for. He had led a charmed life, so far. Born in Berlin in 1908 to a wealthy

Bacalan

Rue Lucien Faure, near the U-Boat submarine pens, Bordeaux, France

CLAUDE MOREAU NODDED POLITELY, feigning interest in what her lover was saying. She had heard this story before, and many others like it – they were invariably boring. Stories about the sea, sailing and the north coast of Germany in winter were of no interest to her, but she concealed it well; she had to.

She was striking to look at, with dark auburn hair, a symmetrical face, blue eyes, full lips and high cheekbones. Her complexion was fair and slightly freckled, with fine laughter lines around her eyes when she smiled. She smiled often: a look of amusement was her natural expression, except when she was angry, and then her eyes were like fire. That it was best not to cross her, was the unspoken consensus. She had no default expression for ennui either; enduring the tedium of repetition was a necessary chore in the line of duty.

She lay back under the bedclothes of an antique hand-carved

again, I had played right into his skillful hands. But I knew in my heart his words were sincere.

*

I was irritated and angered at the ease with which Brim had manipulated me. He was a sapient and resourceful gambler, but a thought had been lurking at the back of my mind about something he'd said with reference to the course at Beaulieu:

Watch your back.

I now realised that he had said this to warn me about the 'Test': the dawn interrogation by the faux Gestapo officers. He had warned me, and he need not have. In fact, he obviously shouldn't have. It explained Freddie's surprise visit and the book so carefully placed in the back of the Alvis. A gift from Brim, he had said without explanation.

Now I was on my way. The network was to be named MONKEYPUZZLE, and I would be dropped near Tours by an RAF Lysander to meet the network organiser, Raymond Flower (Gaspard). My codename was SCORPIUS, but Brim always referred to me as The Artist, and that suited me fine.

From now on, I would be somebody else.

and ground it so hard the tray spun around. “Find him. Seduce him. Ask him about U-Boat 123. We want to know more detail. And then...”

“What, terminate him – is that the vernacular? After having gained his trust and convinced him I was a menial shop assistant?” I breathed deeply; this was not what I had expected: Seduction and assassination was to be my mission.

“There is no one else, Lucy.”

I laughed; I couldn’t help it: “Did you know this moment would come when we had tea with Freddie at the Savoy that day? The day I signed the Official Secrets Act for King and country?”

He took a judicious moment before answering: “Yes. Not necessarily Heller, but someone similar. You are a very beautiful woman, Lucy.”

“Stop,” I blasted out angrily. “Please don’t patronise me. I think I’m grown up enough to understand the game of betrayal. I’ll do it.” It was as quick as that. And I knew I would, without question, because of Tommy and whatever fate he had met at the hands of the Gestapo. Not to mention Freddie in his burning cockpit; and all the others I had met.

“Good.” He stood and held out his hand, which I took. But instead of merely shaking it, he held onto it. “You are an exceptional agent – part of a unique breed, Lucy - and that is not being patronising. It is true. As brave and courageous as any soldier or airman. Freddie was completely right about you.” He released my hand, smiled and looked me in the eye.

Flotilla. Their mission is to torpedo and destroy shipping in the North Atlantic. Those are Hitler's orders, carried out by Admiral Karl Dönitz."

"I see." I visualised the picture of Dönitz I had seen at Norgeby House and listened as Brimblecombe continued.

"There is one U-Boat Commander we are very interested in. His name is Commander Dieter Heller, and he has nine patrols under his command. He has created a record for carnage and death at sea: 34 Allied ships sunk carrying US troops, supplies and food. ..." Brimblecombe paused. "But for all that violence, it turns out the Commander has, ah yes, a predilection for le vin rouge." He made it sound like a weakness for choir boys or opium. Possibly both.

I sensed what was coming: "So that's why I spent two weeks working with Jean-Claude Bodinaud, your sommelier friend from Dégustation Restaurant? Learning the finer points of Grand Cru?"

Brimblecombe gave a deep and heartfelt sigh. "Yes, we know Heller has more than a penchant for fine Bordeaux. Médoc and Pomerol are his tipples, shall we say. One of SCIENTIST's local assets has found you a suitable position in a shop in the Chartrons district of town: Rue Ramonet. Heller goes there regularly. Actually, it's more than a shop: the Germans have arranged tastings – for higher Nazi ranks - and visits to various vineyards. Even excursions to The Grande Champagne area around Segonzac to sample Pineau des Charentes."

I stared at his back as he paused, “And?”

“Suffice it to say, Lucy, that it didn’t happen.” He went on to say that in January 1942 an agent, Robert Leroy, had returned to London via Spain bringing with him valuable information from inside Bordeaux docks with details of useful French contacts that would soon form the SOE SCIENTIST circuit.

“Useful in that they were prepared to be of assistance?” I asked, feeling I needed to know as much as possible.

Brimblecombe turned. “Yes, and more.” Leroy, Brim reported, returned to Bordeaux in June 1943 where he was assigned Bassens, a residential district adjacent to the River Garonne, as his target area. “There is no doubt that SCIENTIST’s agents and contacts in the heart of the docks provided essential intelligence about German activity and local assets; a view supported by Vera Atkins, F Section Intelligence Officer and assistant to Colonel Maurice Buckmaster ...” He paused a moment ... and looked at me closely ...

“I gather you met them at Beaulieu?”

“Yes, they were most gracious,” I said, remembering my cheeky quip about the lack of certificate.

Brimblecombe returned to his seat, took out his cigarette case and lit a Senior Service.“Anyway, a confidential report was written in ’43 assessing the work of the SCIENTIST network in Bordeaux and what it had achieved. It covered bombing, mining the Gironde, and sabotaging German shipping.”

“Quite a lot, it seems.”

Brief

British Intelligence HQ, London, England.

A FEW DAYS LATER, I was summoned to Professor Brimblecombe's office. He was at his most avuncular and made me feel very welcome. After the small talk was over, he explained that Freddie had returned to Switzerland to meet up with his brother, Alistair. Then Brimblecombe's demeanour became serious and I knew something was up.

"Bordeaux, as you know, is a vital port offering access to the Atlantic, and it has long been the subject of SOE interest. In the summer of '43 a U-Boat bunker was completed with eleven pens in all, but I'll come to that in a moment." He stood, turned around to look out of his window to admire one or two plants he had carefully nurtured. "Before that, in September '41, two RF Section agents were dropped south and west of Bordeaux to make contact with potential resistants. Their mission was to identify future targets – particularly around the German aerodrome at Mérignac – and recce possible air-landing grounds

place – it has been a battle of nerves between Mr. Churchill and Hitler."

"Sir," I agreed, looking from one to the next. So, my report had been of some use. My mission not a complete waste of time. What, I wondered, had Pascale reported after our meeting at the Gare du Nord?

"Rest assured that every effort will be made to find out who betrayed Lieutenant Yeo-Thomas and, more importantly, why. He is a damned good man, an asset to SOE; just as you are."

"Silk and cyanide," said Leo Marks finally. "The former may save your life one day. Let's pray you never need the latter." His brown eyes shone with mischief.

I had no idea how prophetic those words would prove to be, but I heard Brimblecombe say: "She won't," as I stood to leave the meeting.

Initially there was no mention of Tommy, the fiasco in Paris or anything pertaining to my hastily aborted mission, but I could feel something palpable in the air. I sensed I was being tested and that the Seahorse mission had been designed to see how I coped under pressure, threat and conflict. And continuous danger.

"At ease, Ensign Fry," said Gubbins formally. He had a blunt moustache and wore his army uniform; the others were in civvies. He was studying some papers in a familiar cardboard SOE file; there was a coffee ring on the back of the file, and I knew who had put it there. 'An innocent trademark', one of the trainers at Grendon (Station 53/Signals) had told me, 'and it may come in handy one day'. I had disregarded the remark at the time; now I almost smiled, but the occasion felt too serious. "Your record is enviable, Ensign Fry. Marks here says you are a natural with codes and ciphers – let alone the Times crossword." He grunted as he read some more. "And your French; well, let's say everyone is impressed."

Brimblecombe chipped in, "We have a very special mission for you, Lucy. It's fraught with danger, but we believe you are perfect for it. I'll fill you in with the details later."

"Thank you, sir." I would later reflect upon those three words with which I effectively committed myself.

Gubbins cleared his throat. "We have read your report about Paris, Ensign Fry. It was the right decision to come back to London. Professor Brimblecombe will debrief you fully on that

glasses. She tapped my knee under the table, I could feel the sharp corners of a stiff envelope. I looked at her quizzically.

"Money and rail tickets," she explained.

"I don't need..."

This time it was she who cut me off in mid flow.

"What you need, Mademoiselle, is to be out of Paris." She pointed at the impressive entrance to the Gare du Nord. "There is a train due to depart in nineteen minutes. That's why I suggested we meet here. Be sure you are on it."

I took the envelope and put it in my bag without even looking at it. Pascale swigged her wine and put the tumbler back on the metal table. A red rim of lipstick remained: it looked like a half-demonic smile. She stood up from the chair and frowned. "We'll find out who did this to Tommy. I just pray he didn't have to suffer."

With that she turned and was gone. I looked at the station clock; I knew I had to be on that train. I left a few coins on the table and walked away.

*

Such was my brief excursion to Paris, but I made it back home safely. A few days later, I was summoned to Norgeby House in London. Major-General Colin Gubbins had been the Director of SOE since August 1943. He sat in his cluttered office with Professor Brimblecombe and the cryptographer, Leo Marks,

French ID. She seemed suspicious of me even though she knew I'd spent time and had been trusted by the Rouen network. She was senior staff at BCRA and understandably nervous. She prayed that Yeo-Thomas had taken his 'L' tablet (cyanide) before they realised who he really was.

The café was thick with cigarette smoke, but it wasn't the tobacco from before the war. This was cow dung and wood shavings, or whatever it was, foul even to an ex-smoker. "I don't feel comfortable here," Pascale said, almost looking over her shoulder to make sure we were not overheard. This was so different to London, because absolutely no one could be trusted. The most innocent-looking person could be an informer. I nodded. "In view of what's happened to Yeo-Thomas you must return to England, now. Go to Boulogne or Calais. I can organise for a Wireless Operator to send London a signal to let them know your mission is aborted. At least you can report what happened here."

"No signal. One betrayal is enough for one day."

"What do you mean?" She snapped.

"I mean Yeo-Thomas was betrayed. Things are not right."

Her eyes blazed with anger and contempt: "You don't think I ...?"

I cut her off and softened my tone. "No not you, Pascale. I didn't mean to imply anything. I'm sorry if you thought I did."

"Alright." She looked around again; uneasy and self-conscious.

among French people. Dieppe was his hometown, and he had been company secretary to a world-renowned Paris fashion house, a testament to his abilities as a networker. Just as the war broke out he joined the RAF and later became known to the SOE, RF Section. It was clear to them that he would be most useful returning to Paris and reassuming the identity of a well-connected French businessman whilst working undercover.

In February 1944, Yeo-Thomas was flown from RAF Tempsford and parachuted back into France. My mission was to meet him and a member of the Bureau Central de Renseignements et d'Action (BCRA) – the Free French intelligence agency. There was one key question that needed an answer: how much the Germans knew about Operation Overlord – the planned Allied invasion of Nazi-occupied France scheduled to take place in June of that year.

I arrived in Paris – via my own drop-in to an airfield near Rouen – to find that all hell had broken loose. I learned that Yeo-Thomas had been betrayed and captured at Passy Metro Station. It was thought by his colleagues at BCRA that he had been abducted by the Gestapo and taken to their headquarters in the Rue des Saussaies. There was an eye-witness account of his arrest, but that was all my contacts knew. It was likely, they surmised, that he would be held at Fresnes Prison and tortured for information. From there, who knows? – probably Buchenwald or another concentration camp.

This left me in an invidious position, wondering what to do. I

Seahorse

Gare du Nord, Paris, France.

IT WAS NOW FEBRUARY 1944, some four months since I had keeled over backwards off the boat into the freezing loch. That all seemed a very long time ago; the training had been exhausting, but I knew I had the support of Brim, Freddie and all my senior officers at SOE.

I'd had an initial mission into occupied Belgium, where there was concern about British codes being broken by the Germans. There had been similar breaches of security in Holland and Denmark, to which I would not be assigned because of the language barrier. Dutch and Danish were definitely not in my skillset.

My second assignment that month was far more significant; and eventually descended into tragedy. I had been instructed to travel to Paris to meet Flight Lieutenant Forest Frederick Yeo-Thomas, codenamed Seahorse by SOE and White Rabbit by the Gestapo. The man was a legend in the Intelligence community.

twenty-four.

*

And that's how it all started. I had been thoroughly trained and became one of theirs, an SOE agent. I had already handed my notice in to Queen Victoria Hospital – Sally Brooke wasn't in the least bit surprised – and my life changed forever.

On my last day in Beaulieu, I was standing in the panelled reception area of the main house waiting for transport when a door opened, and two people came out, dressed in civilian clothing. It was the woman who spoke first. She addressed me with authority.

"I'm Vera Atkins and this is Colonel Buckmaster, head of F Section."

He was tall, with prominent blue eyes and a confident manner. He smiled warmly at me.

"We hear very good things about you, Ensign Fry. You have passed the course with distinction." He held out his hand, which I shook. "The trouble is, we can't give you a certificate. You'll just have to take our word for it."

"That's all right, sir," I found myself saying, "I never was one for paperwork; I'm more of a doer."

The two of them laughed and I thought: Well now, I really am in the inner circle. What a pity Freddie wasn't there to witness it.

The Gestapo men pulled off their caps, perspiration running down their faces, which changed in an instant. They seemed very disturbed by the theatre they'd been instructed to perform.

Another man came in, dressed in a white jacket and holding a clip board. His expression was grave. "I am your conducting officer, follow me." He took my arm and led me into a warm room that was like a clinic. I was shaking like a leaf. "You did well." He sat me on a leather couch and looked at me: "Are you all right?"

I wanted to scream at him and say: No I am not bloody well all right. I am absolutely terrified.

"What happened here tonight was what might happen if you ever got caught by the Nazi scum who occupy France. You have been chosen because of your love of that country, and for your desire to see Britain win this war." He paused and gave me a chance to absorb his words. "As far as we are concerned, you are outstanding as an agent. Are you sure you want to carry on?"

I thought of Freddie in his flaming Tiger Moth, trapped in the cockpit, sure he would be burned alive. 'Yes, Lucy old thing, of course you want to carry on,' he would have said. 'Bloody well show them you can do it.' But all I could manage was a nod. I was drained.

"Right," said the conducting officer, "back to your lodge for a bit more kip. Sound all right?"

"Yes," I said finally and stood. The room swirled for a moment, and then I focused on a clock on the wall. It was exactly

have Churchill's balls and the King's neck in a noose.

"Climb down and sit on the stool." I did as I was bid and suddenly it went dark, the voices dissolved into silence. I was alone and freezing. I don't know how long I sat there. More than five hours, possibly six. It was harrowing and disorientating. Suddenly a lamp shone in my eyes; it was blinding and shocking. A man came from behind and forced my mouth open. He was wearing rubber gloves and I could feel his quick breath on my cheek; hot and rank with tobacco. I could hear a bag being opened and surgical instruments being selected.

"Scalpel!" My body tensed; a rope was tied around my arms. I started to struggle, but it was no use. I was overwhelmed. "Cut her mouth, at both corners, before we start. And get the tourniquet; she'll talk eventually, they always do." There was a shriek of laughter from the men. Then the man's face was near mine again. I could feel a cold blade caressing my top lip.

"What is your name?" This was a Berlin accent; I could tell by its harshness.

"Claude Moreau. I live in Paris. Clignancourt. Rue ..."

The leather glove was slapped across my face again, harder this time. "No. You are English. I think we should arrange transport to Germany. Send her to Dachau; teach her a lesson."

There was more laughter: "They say the stink of piss and shit is unbearable." Another said: "Yes. Human excrement and decaying flesh. Most of them have TB."

"And syphilis."

deliberately bad German.

Another man came in, stone-faced, and ripped the drawer out of the cabinet. He found my French ID card – always referred to as a CNI – among my personal belongings, stockings, underwear. The intrusion was unbearable. Had the facility been breached?

"Put your dressing gown on," the first man snarled at me, looking at my semi-naked body with undisguised lust. I noticed he had a machine gun slung over his shoulder. I couldn't look him in the eye, I was shaking. I did as he had instructed me and stood. The man dragged me out of the lodge into the cold night air. I wasn't wearing either shoes or slippers; tiny shards of gravel punctured the soles of my feet. The man was brutal, pushing and shoving me. Then we were on soft grass. It was pitch black. I felt myself being directed onto a pathway and then down stone steps. Where was I? We descended into a basement full of men, all wearing Gestapo uniform denoting varying ranks. In the middle of the room was a kitchen table and stool.

"Stand on the table!" a man shouted. His black collar patch and SD sleeve insignia identified him as Sturmbandführer. I climbed up onto the stool and then onto the table. The men started laughing; I was shaking with fear and humiliation, anticipating gang rape and torture, then death. I could hear them talking about one of the trainers: Michael, a lock-picker. How they had slit his throat, how he had bled like a pig. How he hadn't seen it coming. Call this a British Intelligence safe house?

He also quizzed me on the arrondissement system: a level of administration created after the French Revolution. I was surprised at how much I remembered from school.

Before he left, he opened the boot of the Alvis and produced a small rectangular parcel. I tore off the wrapping to reveal a copy of La Maison du Juge, a detective novel by Georges Simenon. One of my uncles in Normandy had several of the Maigret novels, and I had worked my way along his bookshelves when visiting, but this title was new to me. On the flyleaf were the initials: P.A.D.

"A gift from Brim," he said without explanation.

"Does this mean I am now a member of the inner circle, Freddie?" I asked him, repacking the book and placing it my bag.

"Yes, Lucy old thing, I suppose it does."

*

It was 3am when I heard a click as my bedroom door opened. I always sleep on my left-hand side and found myself staring at the alarm clock. A tall, fair-haired man wearing a senior-rank Gestapo uniform, leather jackboots and a sidearm came over to my bedside. Was it a dream? I was so befuddled with sleep that I couldn't tell. Had someone drugged my cocoa last night? He grabbed my arm and dragged me out of bed, shouting in German: "Where is your identity card? What is your name?" He slapped me across the face with a leather glove. The sting was

Lymington, Brockenhurst and the Splash at Sway. It was January but a winter sun shone, the roof was down and cosy blankets covered our legs. We stopped for lunch at the Red Lion at Boldre. The ponies seemed to roam freely around the forest roads. One even came into the pub and showed a lot of interest in the pastie on Freddie's plate until it was shooed out by an embarrassed landlord.

"I have to return to Switzerland," he said as we arrived back at Beaulieu, "but I just wanted to see you."

"One last time?" I chided him.

"Don't be silly. To wish you good luck."

"Do you know where they are sending me, Freddie?" I took hold of his arm.

"France?"

He smiled and raised his eyebrows the way he always did. For twenty minutes we conversed in French and my rather lackluster German. I could certainly understand it better than I could speak it. And that was despite some intensive tuition from an SOE language instructor. Freddie went on to ask me some tricky questions I wasn't prepared for. Some were about the names of former French presidents and exactly where certain French towns and cities were located. And where exactly is the source of the river Charente?

"The Haute-Vienne département at Chéronnac, a small village near Rochechouart. And it flows into the Atlantic Ocean near Rochefort." I replied with confidence. I didn't have to dig

As part of the security training, we learned to recognise the ranks of the ordinary French police, and of the more dangerous uniformed French Milice. We were taught to distinguish the different ranks of the ordinary German soldiers. We also needed to know about the branches of German counterintelligence, though it was hoped that we would never encounter them. The SD was the intelligence wing of the SS: the political state police, which also controlled the Gestapo. The SD and the military Abwehr were fiercely opposed to one another, and it was rumoured that the Abwehr would be absorbed by the SS.

*

On the thirteenth day of the New Forest Fortnight – as we four girls had nicknamed it – I had the surprise of my life: Freddie Valentine appeared on the drive outside the main house in an open-topped Alvis tourer. Due to his prosthetic leg he was unable to drive, so he'd requisitioned the services of a fully liveried chauffeur.

I was sitting quietly in my lodge writing a letter to my father in Devon when a telephone call came through from reception. "A gentleman to see you, Ensign Fry," said one of the staff, rather stuffily. I charged out of my door like a rocket.

"Lucy, old thing! Surprised?" he said. He was dressed in a tweed jacket and plus fours and, only needed a gun and the dogs to make him look the epitome of an English gentleman ready for

Beaulieu

Group B finishing school, Hampshire, England.

THE FINAL FEW WEEKS of my training took place at Beaulieu in Hampshire, one of the Group B finishing schools. The course was designed to enable students to catch their breath and enjoy the tranquillity of the Abbey cloisters as well as completing the academic and physical tasks. I saw it as a welcome break, with walks in the New Forest and a chance for me to do some sketching; a hobby I had neglected because of the SOE workload. This part of the course brought us back into the classroom to learn the finer points of security and espionage. "Knowledge," one of our trainers often said, "is paramount to your safety".

We were housed in small cottages known as 'The Lodges', a stone's throw away from the main house. The days were structured but casual; mealtimes in the main dining room were communal – one could eat in their lodge, alone, but none of the four of us chose to do so. The regime suited us and our conversations were always bland; no personal information was

it my imagination, or did I feel something that felt like canvas webbing being tightened around my waist? I couldn't move an inch: I was a prisoner.

"Breathe normally through your nose now, nice and deep, that's it," said Jackson, his voice drifting away into the distance. My world sank into a kaleidoscopic series of images: Devon and Normandy. East Grinstead.

room. I am sure I could detect specks of blood on his pocket, unless he owned a leaky fountain pen.

I sat down in the chair and tried to relax. The surgery smelt of ether and other chemical agents which were as familiar to me as they were frightening. Jackson explained he would be using pure nitrous oxide administered through a rubber face mask for anaesthesia. He held up a rubber contraption through which I would establish nasal respiration. My mouth would be occupied by a throat pack, and Beryl's delicate instruments, one presumed. "Then it will be gas and oxygen," said Jackson, "a subtle blend of both, which I deliver through this." He pointed at a Boyle's anaesthetic machine: a trolley-like apparatus consisting of tubes and cylinders of compressed air and gases; a contraption I was very familiar with from my nursing days. I nodded and looked at the good doctor with a question:

"What if I don't have any English fillings? Much of my childhood was spent in France. They probably are French," I said in desperation; I was starting to panic.

"That's for me to discover. There will certainly be other dental issues, there always are. Dr. Jackson when you are ready, please."

"Yes, Beryl," he said quietly.

"Sit back and relax, young lady. Base of the spine against the back of the chair and open wide please. There is a nice Constable on the ceiling on which you might like to focus. A calming Suffolk scene. There, that's good. Wider, please!"

Dentist

Harley Street, London, England.

THERE WERE NO INTRODUCTIONS. I suppose there couldn't be. Freddie remained out in the waiting room clutching a hefty book, which I took as a bad sign.

"Do you have fillings?" asked Dr. Beryl Murray-Davies. Her voice was clipped and businesslike; she seemed to be examining me before the procedure even started.

"Yes." In fact, I couldn't remember the last time I had seen a dentist. "Probably."

"I have to make sure none of your fillings are of English origin. If they are, I must replace them with continental amalgam replicas."

"I see, but..."

She took a breath which I took to indicate impatience: "Sit down, young lady. This is Dr. Andrew Jackson, an anaesthetist with whom I am conducting research for a clinical paper. It's all right, he doesn't bite." She chuckled at her own joke, which I

Brimblecombe stood; his business done; my commitment complete.

"Yes." I watched Brimblecombe carefully; I could imagine he possessed the rhetorical skills to deal with politicians and senior military personnel with equal skill.

"The Secret Intelligence Service has a distinct role: liaising with signals and codes; assigning agents in Europe who monitor and report the situation in, say, France. It is a passive role. Mr. Churchill's words were to set Europe ablaze as far as SOE is concerned. SOE is active, and its role is subversion. Part of it, at least." Brimblecombe delivered what passed for a smile.

He went on to say that SOE had become the first organisation in the history of British warfare with a licence to commit sabotage. It was responsible for conducting all forms of clandestine warfare, building up secret armies in occupied territories and securing maximum co-operation from governments-in-exile. SOE's quota of aircraft, arms and essential supplies would be substantially increased. This would give rise to a sharp increase in 'dropping operations' – in other words, parachuting from an aircraft into occupied territory. Every mission would carry a huge personal risk; some would be more sensitive than others. I was asked if this was clear.

"Perfectly clear, sir."

"Before you commence operational work out in the field, there is much to do. Firstly, there is someone else you need to meet."

"Oh?" I enquired innocently.

"Her name is Beryl Murray-Davies: delightful lady. They call

Retrieval Test'. I am told it is the most gruelling challenge of the course. Only four out of ten make it."

I looked at Freddie. "Not terribly good odds: forty percent?"

He gave me an encouraging smile: "No. It's a long way from East Grinstead. But we wouldn't have asked if we didn't think you could do it. The potholing incident you told me about at – where was it – Cheddar? Made me cringe."

"Yes; well, I wouldn't do it again."

Brimblecombe continued: "Finally, there's Finishing School at Beaulieu in the New Forest in Hampshire. Wireless training, microphotography, lock-picking and safe-breaking, and..." He glanced across at Freddie, "watching your back." The two men were blank-faced and, before I could ask what he meant, he continued. "The point is, Lucy," said Brimblecombe, "there are thousands of young women like you: FANYs doing outstanding work for this country against a tyrannical Nazi regime. These are difficult and unprecedented times. SOE has parachuted countless agents – male and female – into occupied France. You'll be part of a covert unit. There is no question but that you possess the attributes."

"Courage and loyalty," put in Freddie. "Attributes that can't be taught. Instinct."

Brimblecombe became even more serious: "He's right. I sense it."

"Thank you."

A hint of a smile crossed his face: "Now, what I am about to

I'd sign the OSA. He'd brought the documents, and Freddie had brought the pen. Never mind bait; this was hook, line and sinker. And I was caught.

*

A second tray of tea was served by Sandra and her colleague, followed by gin and tonics. But this was all to prepare me for what was to come: my brief.

"Now then, let me explain in more detail what this is all about," said Brimblecombe. "Firstly, you'll undergo vigorous instruction at a Commando school in Scotland. They call it Guerrilla Training. You won't be able to tell anyone where you are going or why – and that includes your parents, I'm afraid. Oh, don't look so disappointed!"

"Sorry."

Brimblecombe pressed on: "The course is demanding; I won't mislead you. Brutal, some would say. You'll learn about encryption and codes with the excellent Leo Marks; sabotage, explosives, hand-to-hand combat, weapons and firearms: all the specialist skills you'll need for covert operations abroad."

"Spying?" I suggested rather feebly, and he almost cut me off.

"Spying is only part of it; we prefer to call it surveillance. The parachute training takes place at Tatton Park, near Manchester. The trainers aim for recruits to do five drops; at least one at night, and later, one with a leg bag for carrying equipment and

understand."Brimblecombe looked me in the eye; he'd somehow made it sound as if I were already under his command and this was merely a formality. His authority was captivating and utterly persuasive: I really felt I had no choice.

I peered over at Freddie, who looked back with his most engaging smile. He was nodding, very slightly. All the words had made sense: duty, honour and fear. And, oh, such excitement. My mind was made up.

"Yes, I'm in." The quick words of acquiescence came out almost as if my mouth belonged to someone else. I sensed an expression of relief on Freddie's handsome features. Brimblecombe withdrew some formal-looking documents from his inside jacket pocket.

"Good. You will need to sign the Official Secrets Act here, witnessed by Freddie, because what I am about to discuss with you is classified. Members of SOE are recruited from all walks of life. All are required to sign the OSA. You are currently a civilian. From the moment you sign this, you are not. Is that clear?"

"Yes." I took the documents, signed and dated them with the fountain pen Freddie apparently produced from nowhere and passed them back to Brimblecombe. He waved the sheets around in the warm air to dry.

"Everything satisfactory, Ensign Fry?" asked Freddie with that discerning grin of his.

"Freddie, what have you got me into?"

"Winning the war, Lucy. Winning this damned war,"

that my immediate and practical response indicated a positive interest.

It was Freddie who answered. “That can be taken care of, Lucy; the main thing here is that you can see why we believe you would be perfect.”

I sighed, speechless, as he continued, “It's not just your language skills, Lucy.” Freddie spoke softly and persuasively. “No. I have seen you work in a crisis at the hospital, where life and death hang in the balance. You are a coper: practical, independent, resourceful. Fearless, I would say. And steely. That’s what we need.”

“The perfect spy,” added Brimblecombe. “All you need is the appropriate training.”

“Training?” The conversation had developed so fast.

“Ever heard of the FANYs?” Brimblecombe asked. He tapped his cigarette case, clearly tempted to light another. He resisted and waited for my response.

“I’ve heard of them.”

“First Aid Nursing Yeomanry closely associated with SOE. You would join with the rank of Ensign – Second Lieutenant in the army. But you’d be under my direct command at British Intelligence. There will be a number of missions to France where SOE and MI6 would operate together...” Brimblecombe paused and looked at me as a headmaster might regard a student as she contemplates her future. “... It’s a lot to take in, I realise. But, are you in? If yes, we continue. If no, I stand and we both leave as if

need to look at Freddie like that, Lucy, really. He was merely doing his job. I imagine you have remained close to your family in France." It was more a statement than a question.

"As close as we can, given the circumstances, yes." By now I suspected what was coming; the bait had been cast and I was being reeled in. Brimblecombe scrunched out his cigarette and his tone chilled me; the avuncular manner vanished.

"Lucy, Adolf Hitler will stop at nothing until France has been bludgeoned into complete capitulation. Europe – all of it – will be ruled by a deluded tyrant unless he is prevented." Brimblecombe eyed me with utter compulsion, and I felt myself swallowing deeply.

"What is this about exactly, sir?" I sounded formal and gave him my gravest face.

He chuckled and pursed his lips. "Oh come now, just a little gentle coercion, Lucy. Nothing drastic. Don't you see? You are ideally placed to accomplish a great deal for France, for your family, and consequently for Great Britain and her allies."

"Me? To do what exactly? I am a nurse in the Burns Unit of a hospital. My job is to look after patients like Freddie here. People with terrible..." I stopped, suddenly realising I was talking in rapid French. Embarrassment must have been written all over my face.

Brimblecombe grinned; it was a curious little expression which passed quickly over his sombre features and vanished in an instant. He glanced at Freddie and said to him in flawless

"You don't hear from Freddie for ages and here you are enjoying tea with him at the Savoy. And then I arrive, out of the blue!" He gave out a little chuckle and looked at me for a response. I probably nodded. He continued, "Freddie tells me you have family in France. Normandy, I believe?"

I was perplexed, and I probably looked it. "Yes. Yes, I do."

"Are you close to them?" I would think later what a strange question that was.

"Yes, very. My cousins and I grew up together for big chunks of my childhood. My mother was ill in England – so I was, well - exported to France. My father couldn't cope with an adolescent daughter who was 'difficult'. One problematic female was enough for him, poor chap.'"

Brimblecombe arched an eyebrow: "Where exactly, may I ask, were you exported to?"

"Mondeville, St-Aubin-sur-Mer and Bayeux; two aunts and uncles; five cousins. My mother's sisters." I looked at Freddie, who acknowledged me sheepishly as I continued. "I attended school in Bayeux for, oh, how long was it, five years? My mother had – has – quite severe mental problems and I am an only child."

"So, in effect, you are half French?" Brimblecombe smoked his cigarette and regarded me carefully. "Is that correct?"

"Yes, I suppose so. Why do you ask?"

Freddie had obviously told him all about me and, in a way, I felt betrayed. I glanced at him again and Brimblecombe must

tea and cake for an hour or so when there was a soft tap on the door, and a stylishly dressed man entered the room. At first I assumed he was a senior member of hotel management. He was in his fifties, five feet eight, stocky in build and not dissimilar to Alfred Hitchcock in appearance. The man had presence and introduced himself in well-modulated tones.

"Good afternoon, Miss Fry," he nodded at Freddie, "I am Nicholas Brimblecombe. Would you mind if I joined you both for a minute?" He glanced again at Freddie in a familiar way, and Freddie smiled back. I must have looked confused. I was confused.

A pair of uniformed waitresses entered the room, wheeling an ornate trolley bearing a silver teapot and bone china cup and saucer. "Your usual, Professor," said one. She bobbed, and I detected a faint blush on the young girl's face. "Earl Grey. No milk or sugar. I'll pour, but I'll give it a jiffy to brew, shall I?"

Brimblecombe nodded, "Thank you, Sandra." He oozed affability and charm. "Most kind." How unusual that he should remember the girl's name. I would learn that this was typical of his attention to detail in everything he did. Freddie watched the scene unfold with detached amusement and sipped his tea. Everything had been planned perfectly. Presently Sandra poured the tea through a strainer and both waitresses withdrew, closing the door quietly behind them. This scene, I felt sure, had been played many times before.

"Now, my dear, I expect you are wondering what this is all

as my French cousins. I knew all their games and the subtle nuances of language. He seemed to be genuinely interested in me, and Sally apparently was unconcerned about our friendship. Maybe she didn't see me as a threat? My relationship with Freddie was almost sisterly; certainly, never sexual. Freddie was tall and lean. And his injury, although debilitating, never seemed to affect his mobility or sense of fun – quite the reverse.

Sometime after Freddie's sudden departure, the ward telephone bulb glowed, and I responded to its insistent signal. I was on an early shift and Ward 3 was quiet. All my patients were either dozing, reading or listening to the wireless. It was Freddie, inviting me to visit him in London. I was taken aback, and I swear my heart missed a beat. I expressed my reservations, and his response was, to be honest, disappointing,

"No, not like that, Lucy old thing! I have an idea to put to you and it really needs to be face- to-face. Give it some thought, and I'll call back in a few days."

I decided to confide in Sally – there was no way that I wouldn't – she was my senior and also my friend. She was perfectly happy for me to meet him on my next day off. It only occurred to me later that Freddie had, of course, cleared it with Sally in the first place.

*

And so I caught the train up to London and met Freddie at

hearts of all the wounded servicemen she nursed. All the Guinea Pigs – the nickname for the patients, who called the ward 'the sty' – were secretly in love with Sally. I was convinced that she and Freddie had a romance; and if they had, they certainly kept it very discreet. But the sty was like that – lots of love affairs. And plenty of rumours.

Shortly afterwards, without warning, Freddie left the hospital and apparently went to London. No explanation was given. Sally was clearly devastated. She obviously admired Freddie for his kindness, integrity, and bravery. Even more than that, she valued his strength, passion, irreverence and sense of humour.

I would miss him too, and I was convinced I would never see him again. I loved Freddie too in my own sort of way, and I was envious of the closeness he shared with Sally. Freddie and I had also spent a lot of time together outside Ward 3 at the local pub – The Guinea Pig – where we were encouraged by McIndoe and his team to go for a change of scene. Freddie had asked an extraordinary number of questions, wanting to know all about my life outside nursing. He questioned me thoroughly about my home, my family and friends, where I stood politically, who I admired, and who I didn't. He made observations about my hobbies: canoeing – "sounds rather dangerous, Lucy old thing"; horse-riding on Dartmoor – "unpredictable beasts"; and deep-water swimming in Cornwall – "I would call that a bit risky".

Long stays with my mother's extended family in Normandy meant that my French was fluent. I'd spent all my school

Recruitment

Savoy Hotel, London, England.

WE RETURNED TO ARISAIG HOUSE, and I was permitted an hour off. I wandered into the canteen and ordered myself a hot chocolate, which I took up to my room. I decided to skip the single malt for now. After a hot bath, I lay down on the tiny single bed and closed my eyes. No matter what, I was always conscious of time and had been for the three weeks I had been here. And oh, what a journey it had been.

Tiny specks floated in the aqueous fluid before my eyes as my mind wandered back to meeting Freddie Valentine for the first time. He'd had a terrible accident in a Tiger Moth biplane and been transferred to the Queen Victoria Hospital in East Grinstead, where I worked as a nurse. My station was the Burns Unit, overseen by Mr. Archibald McIndoe, the renowned reconstructive surgeon.

My senior was a girl called Sally Brooke – a staff nurse on Ward 3. She was a golden-haired, freckle-faced Scot from

Incendiary Grenade stared back at me. It was grey and sinister. I thrust it into the diving bag strapped onto the front of my suit, closed the trunk's lid and re-locked the padlock. As I turned the shackle back and re-engaged the mechanism, I dropped the key.

Forty seconds. And then I spotted it, floating just above the loch bed, suspended in the weed like a dead fish. I grabbed it and swam back up towards the boat, desperate for air, willing myself to stay calm and controlled. Although I'd only dived down to a maximum of sixty feet, I knew I had to ascend gradually and cautiously. My practice dives had not yet included the retrieval test. But now I'd done it.

Finally, my palm brushed against the wooden hull, and then a hand was there, hauling me out of the freezing water. I tore off the diving mask, gasping for air, panting frantically.

Captain Sykes looked at me, deadpan: "That wasn't so bad was it, Lucy?"

"Ensign Fry ..." I struggled for the witty response I had practised in my mind and collapsed onto the deck, breathless. I didn't notice the grenade had fallen out of my diving bag and was rolling across the wooden planks toward the edge of the deck.

Captain Fairburn looked utterly horrified: "Christ! Lucky the bastard wasn't bloody armed, or we'd all have been toasted."

"Aye, on both sides," said Sykes with a grimace.

And then, oblivion. Another box ticked.

darkness. Halfway there.

Thirty feet below in the murky water was the object of my mission: a wooden crate nestling in what looked like a field of undulating weed. It resembled a treasure chest. I clasped a padlock key in my right fist with such determination that I was sure I would drop it. This, too, hampered my ability to swim effectively. It was a nightmare. The one-piece diving mask trapped a volume of air around my eye sockets and nose. It had become slightly askew during my descent and some water had leaked in. I blew a cautious sniff of air through my nose to try and push some of the water out. It worked, thank God. And resealed.

It was desperately cold. I swam deeper, focusing on the crate – twenty feet – ten. I could picture my two instructors above me – in a fishing boat – stopwatches primed as they watched the seconds ticking. Captains Fairburn and Sykes would be worried. I couldn't let them down.

Five more feet and I was there; my knees scraped the bed of the loch, releasing a cloud of debris and bubbles. The padlock looked old and rusty. I tilted it with my left hand until the keyhole was visible. My bare hands were numb with cold, but I needed the tactility. I felt for the indented aperture of the lock with the pad of my thumb and then inserted the key and rotated the oval shackle.

Thirty seconds with no air. I desperately removed the padlock and opened the lid of the trunk, just enough. A few

Lucy Fry, Arisaig House, Lochabar, Scotland

October 1943, British Intelligence Commando Training School.

MY LUNGS WERE BURSTING. I couldn't breathe. I was going to drown; of that, I was certain. I knew I could tolerate danger, but this was something else. Something perilous. And the water was freezing. I dropped further into the darkening abyss. Endless, it seemed, immeasurably deep, my chest tightened. I must push myself further ...

Foul water was starting to seep through my sealed, numb lips and the ancient diving suit did little to disguise the temperature. Plus, it had been made for a man, not an eight-and-a-half stone-woman. The loch darkened more as I descended. I just wanted to get this over and drink a single malt in the bar at Arisaig House. I swam as powerfully as I could, very conscious of my lung capacity ... and time.

The resistance of the water and the awkwardness of my suit impaired both my speed and agility. This underwater world felt

'On July 16, 1940, Prime Minister Winston Churchill appointed a civilian, Hugh Dalton, to be SOE's political master. He then promptly ordered him to

'SET EUROPE ABLAZE!'

First published in the United Kingdom
by TradShack in 2022.

Cover design by www. tradshack.com
Published by www.tradshack.com

ISBN 978-1-7397822-3-8

ROBERT
WALLACE

MONKEYPUZZLE

The third story in the Valentine Series

TradShack

About the Author

Robert Wallace was born and raised in Bristol and spent many years working in the medical field which took him to Europe, the United States, Japan, Australia and Scandinavia. It sparked a lifelong interest in travel. His work involves turning historical events into works of semi-fiction, retaining the factual background, creating fictional characters to share their lives with real people.

Praise for the Author

About 'One *Single Ticket*' by Robert Wallace:

"A detective story told at a breathless pace, with a Richard Hannay type hero straight out of a John Buchan thriller, and it goes with a swing"

Professor Angus Buchanan, author of 'Brunel: The Life and Times of Isambard Kingdom Brunel

"The plot is so interesting, and the setting so well done; a delight to get a scenic picture of this special event in history."

Dr. Gabrielle Obrist, Museum of Modern Art, Zürich

Monkeypuzzle

Also by Robert Wallace

The Valentine Series

Valentines Cup

Crimson Wing

Monkeypuzzle

Operation Gunfleet

Standalone novels

One Single Ticket

A gripping Victorian thriller about Brunel.

Fables and Folk

A collection of urban ghost and mystery stories with factual origins.

The Betrayal of Jacqueline Flower

Andrew is clearly not the man she thought she knew. The man she married.

Printed in Great Britain
by Amazon

50607514R00141